7   2/10
15   8/12
17   5/13

FREAKED

J. T. DUTTON

HARPER TEEN

An Imprint of HarperCollins *Publishers*

ACKNOWLEDGMENTS

I wish to thank my brother, Tim, the faculty, and fellow writers at the University of Alaska; my agent Jodie Rhodes, a courageous woman who was not afraid to discover a new writer; and Alan Trist of Ice Nine Publishing for permission to use lyrics from "Dire Wolf" as an epigraph. Thank you also to the members of the Grateful Dead for inspiring me and their many fans. Finally, thank you, Phoebe Yeh, for your guidance and vision.

Freaked
Copyright © 2009 by J. T. Dutton
Printed in the U.S.A.

This book is a work of fiction and is not intended to be a historical record of real events. Some venues and playlists have been invented for the purpose of charging the story line; others have been described only as I imagined they occurred. Serious historians of the Grateful Dead legacy will note discrepancies, and to them I plead artistic license.

Library of Congress Cataloging-in-Publication Data
Dutton, J. T., date
    Freaked : a novel / J.T. Dutton. — 1st ed.
        p.   cm.
    Summary: In the mid-1990s, Grateful Dead fan Scotty Loveletter must wade through the privileged world of his East Coast prep school while dealing with his absent mother, a famous sex therapist.
    ISBN 978-0-06-137079-3 (trade bdg.)
    [1. Preparatory schools—Fiction.   2. High schools—Fiction.   3. Schools—Fiction.
4. Grateful Dead (Musical group)—Fiction.   5. Mothers and sons—Fiction.]   I. Title.
PZ7.D948Fr   2009   2008024640
[Fic]—dc22   CIP
                                                            AC

Typography by Alison Klapthor
1 2 3 4 5 6 7 8 9 10
❖
First Edition

To Jeff
I love you

When I awoke, the Dire Wolf
Six hundred pounds of sin
Was grinning at my window
All I said was "come on in."
—Robert Hunter, "Dire Wolf"

RIPPLE

AT STILLWATER ACADEMY FOR BOYS, names were one way to calculate the score. A guy with a first name and a last name that sounded like a first name— Kenny James, for example—had a trust fund and a couple of summer homes. A first name that sounded like a last name and a last name meant first-generation cash— electronics in the home and American-made cars like Mustangs. Every once in a while, you met someone with a hyphen, a guy with a last-name first name, last name, and another last name. Davis Richardson-MacArthur— that was a guy with real problems. Those with a first name and a last name were on scholarship, for the most part, but at least their lives were normal. I was a guy with a couple of first names and a bunch of hyphens and my mother's alias. I had so many names, I didn't know who I was. Scotty Emerson-Fitzgerald-Douglas-Loveletter, for Christ's sake.

Then there's Jerome John Garcia—what the hell kind of name is that? It's not Hispanic and it's not Irish either, and Jerry Garcia sounds like the sober handle of a hard-driving captain on a police show, a character with a big heart and a case of schizophrenia written into him in order to provide new stories for the series. But he's what kept me going during the sluggish fall of 1993, my second sophomore year at Stillwater Academy for Boys. He's what raised me up from the funk I had fallen into after finding out my mother wanted to be the 1994 New Year's centerfold, what Kenny J.—one of my buddies— and a thousand other guys just like him stuffed under their beds when some dude barged into their room without knocking. My mother is a hot number, a well-known sex self-help therapist, and she liked on occasion to show that off. Jerry's sunshine daydreams and Aiko Aiko all day, the sweet lilt of Jerry's voice were like a mellow pill that eased me out when I was stressing over the complications of what it was like to be her son for the two and a half years I spent as a Stillwaterite.

I had experienced golden afternoons before I discovered the magical, beautiful music of the Grateful Dead, of course, when I was young and hopeful, when my mother was still an aspiring unknown and I was untouched by her forays into a public life. When I was seven or eight, I owned a pony named Chocolate and a toy sports car. I had even made necessary and sometimes painful adjustments as I got older that didn't kill me, like not sleeping with stuffed animals or sucking my thumb. But like a lot of guys in my income bracket, boarding school was my mother's only option as soon as the answers to my questions required more parental ingenuity than she was willing to spend on one kid.

Stillwater Academy for Boys was a last-resort school for guys like my roommate, Todd, who had gotten kicked out of better schools—Tabor, Taft, and Choate—and guys like me, who, because my mother was Linda Loveletter, advice giver and centerfold, never really stood a chance in the first place. From my first days at Stillwater, I got beat up between classes, bumped into in the hallways, hip-checked at lunch when I was carrying a tray full of sundries, described along with my mother on the backs of bathroom stall doors, made fun of in English class when

I offered up an unusually creative answer about a book I hadn't read, or mocked in math class when I didn't bother being creative and just came off as stupid.

I could be a smart-ass on occasion, and the reason I could be a smart-ass was because every few seconds some hormonal asshole asked me if he could date my mother. But the humiliation didn't stop there. She often talked lovingly about me on her radio show just before giving some schmo a play-by-play on wicked number seven of the eighteen no-fail ways to make a woman sing. She appeared on most of the morning talk shows, every so often offering interesting opinions to people who loved feet, wore handcuffs, or stuck needles through their nose.

When I first got to Stillwater, in my desperation I palled around with just about anybody, which meant *Star Trek* junkies and computer geeks and the like, and gave my assigned roommate a wide berth because he was always inviting upperclassmen into our room, people who knew his brother through the network that connected Stillwater to Taft to Choate, linking the East Coast schools all the way up to Harvard, Dartmouth, Yale, and if a guy messed up some, Amherst. At different times of day, different sets of strangers showed up to buy or smoke Todd's dope. At first, I was harassed as a way to keep me from ratting them all out, but after a while I was ignored, then little by little treated the way a stray dog might have been, getting tossed a few scraps here and there and made to do funny tricks.

By the spring semester of my freshman year, Todd no longer saw me as such a sad, sloppy zero. He force-fed me my first hit of dope. The smoke inflated my already pathetic brain cells and awoke my chi, but what really got me going was the music that was on the deck, Jerry singing "Dear Prudence." I was flattered that a guy with tastes like Todd's wanted to hang out with me, and to prove it, I went ahead and took too much acid, drank rum, risked my SAT scores the same way people risk their physical bodies, all just to be a hero or at least a sidekick in somebody else's eyes, all to get a little closer to the music. By doing the fucked-up things that nobody else would do, I became known around school as a freak with superpowers. I spent a lot of nights kicked back in bed, my brain matter swirling, digesting the Velveeta pepper jack cheese and crickets Todd and his friends had dared me to eat and letting Jerry soothe my soul.

My first close encounter with Saint Jerry was the

1991 Saratoga show. Todd dragged me along on one of his mystery outings. I wore a polo shirt, for Christ's sake. A Goofus maneuver, I admit, but it didn't keep me from enjoying the scene the way it would have a square like Gallant. The band played "Uncle John's Band" right into "Man Smart, Woman Smarter," and then they did this bitching rendition of "Bertha." During the second set, some dude from the freak brigade jumped off the second tier, arms out, tie-dye spread. He fluttered like a fucked-up robin off to meet Jesus, landed on the crowd, curled into a ball, and ran away. Bobby sang "I Need a Miracle" and everybody sang right along with him, dancing like snakes just loose from a box. Todd made a bootleg tape of the Saratoga show and sold me a copy for nine dollars and seventy-five cents. When I slip it into the deck, I can hear a surge from the faithful as the guy falls. Listening to the Saratoga tape is like being transformed all over again without the smell of incense and patchouli, without forty thousand people leaning over me and interfering with the microcosmic implosion of my brain cells.

Since that day in Saratoga, I have lived my life according to all the rules of Jerryism. I have shared my women (if my mother counts) and I have shared my wine (sometimes out the car window or all over my shirt and shoes). I have kept on trucking and smiled, smiled, smiled. In the early days—my first year at Stillwater—I didn't know much about Jerry, about his heroin addiction, his missing finger, his four wives, his kids. All I ever heard about Jerry was his hippie mystery, his beauty, his sainthood, and I basked in the light of it. Jerry's greatest gift to me was his music and the dope that I smoked from doobies, bongs, and (once when I was in a pinch) a carved-out cucumber. Every bit of delirium helped.

One Friday afternoon, when I had made it a few months into my sophomore year a second time, some dude from the hockey team named Gordie or Captain America or some damn thing knocked on our door and asked if he could come in. It was likely going to be someone from the high-testosterone set who found out about my mother's impending nudity first and got it circulating around the school. At Stillwater, there were the usual circles: hockey players, honor students, geeks, and the entertainment committee (whose members were really geeks, too, but didn't think so). Todd was a freak and so was Kenny J., but Todd had the ability to join in a game of chess or a scrimmage of kill-the-guy-with-the-football without giving away that he really had tie-dye tucked under his khaki. I'd even seen Todd hanging around the head table at dinner, talking up the faculty, kidding around with them about baseball scores and basketball games and things nobody gives a damn about anyway but that greased the wheels around grade-averaging time.

It was Todd who had drawn Captain James Tiberius Puckwhacker, or whatever his name was, into our abode. I was the worst for remembering who people were, even though the administration bantered the guy's reputation about plenty when they were fired up about sports programs and athleticism. Like Todd, he appeared to be one of those bound-for-glory types, in his case headed for Dartmouth or Middlebury to do some more puckwhacking, but unlike Todd, he didn't have a brother who sold him dope in retail quantities. He didn't have a double life hiding under his good looks and a roommate with a four-hundred-dollar allowance ripe for the plucking. I'm not saying Todd learned to love me for my ready cash or my sexy mother, but when it came to our differences, his anal-retentive cleanliness and my more laid-back approach to things like hangers, having a few bucks, and Linda on my side definitely helped ease the pain and keep us unilateral.

We made Captain Puckwhacker wait just outside the door while Todd kicked the scale he was weighing dope with under his bed. I went to sit at my desk, and when the guy came in I was drawing on my stepfather's annual report brochure, adding little round glasses and a Day-Glo beard to his picture. The Captain had to flick a pair of my tighty whities off his just-shined penny loafers to cross the distance from our door to the center of the room. A garden of dirty white and tie-dyed underwear sprouted like Jerry's roses all over the carpet. I had stopped using my bureau around midterm, when the stress of late fall had ebbed the mental coordination it took to fold, and I had lapsed into a dirty laundry inertia. Todd had grown patient with the condition. He rolled everything back over to my side when it spilled over the invisible line dividing the Mount Everest of my stuff from the Sahara of his.

"What's up?" Todd asked our visitor.

Instead of wearing the school blazer, Captain Puckwhacker had on an L.L.Bean sweater, a variation on the uniform allowed after five o'clock on Fridays or on guys who had scored more than fifteen points in one season.

At Stillwater, handshaker suits were part of the picture—blue blazers, oxford shirts, ties, khaki pants. On most guys, the Stillwater uniform was a preppy mask designed to keep the folks back home happy and hopeful, convinced of eventual indoctrination into the corporate Nazi world outside.

In the suit, Todd and the Captain looked exactly like the boys old Henry Stillwater, the school founder, had envisioned when he got into the boarding school business. Their ties fit their necks and they never had green stains on their pants from being thrown into the ornamental shrubbery on a regular basis. And even though Todd's eyes swelled from the dope he smoked, it looked like he had spent the night studying instead of hosting another world-record-setting Bongathon. On me, though, the handshaker suit still looked like the digs of a hungover security guard, a joke that will probably keep the late Henry S. rolling in his grave another century.

I gave some thought to splitting for Kenny J.'s room but instead stayed in my desk chair, trying not to make too much eye contact with Captain Puckwhacker. He passed by the desk and checked out the green and orange I had swirled over my stepfather's chest, the peace sign I had drawn into his fingers. Rising to the surface of the Captain's pupils, like the message on a Magic 8 Ball, was what he thought of me: OUTLOOK POOR, THE ANSWER IS DEFINITELY NO, TRY AGAIN. It was a lot of scorn to bestow on one little freak. Then he turned to Todd and said, "We want to buy some weed."

"We?" I asked.

He was obviously a guy who had been sold the whole "Big-We-Little-i-No-I-in-team" bill of goods. I hated guys like him when they got all royal with the "We" stuff.

"Me and my buddies, you moron," he snarled.

I'd been warning Todd about doing business with untrustworthy elements, and a hockey player in an L.L.Bean sweater was by all means an untrustworthy element. But Todd reached under his bed and revealed the dope. He also pulled out and began assembling the Poltergeist, a four-foot-long hookah his older brother had sent him from Turkey, pointing with its top to a flat place on my unmade bed, motioning for his royal Captain-ness to sit down.

Todd had a lot of extra contraband to play with lately—one half purchased from a bonus guilt check he had received from his parents, who had extended their stay in the Caribbean, the other half purchased from what he had made selling bootleg tapes and Grateful Dead tickets to guys with a weekly allowance. In general, whatever Todd could get his hands on he sold. His supplies arrived every month or so wrapped up in new underwear or socks and tucked into a package from his older brother. He took some of the cash he made to the bank but left a pile of it around to stack and count and reinvest. He kept his pile in a shoe box in the closet. Because I was his biggest investor, I sometimes had a smaller pile of my own next to Haley the goldfish, who lived in a glass bowl under my bed.

After he finished packing the bowl of the Poltergeist, Todd distributed two of the Heinekens we had hidden in our mini-fridge. Captain Puckwhacker accepted everything as if he had been tutored in freak protocol ahead of time. He poured the beer into an empty Coke can and blew the smoke from the dope Todd offered him into an old towel we kept around to keep the stink down. Todd's pot can bring on the paranoia, and something crawled up my back as I watched the Captain go to work on the hookah, holding the tube so that it didn't pinch in the middle and stopping his breath after he had sucked up the smoke. Besides the dope and the unauthorized pet, there was enough other contraband hidden around the room to get us kicked out of Stillwater Academy at any second of any day. Just about anything that was fun was considered contraband. Drugs were considered contraband. So were cigarettes, girls, rattling the windows with a new pair of speakers, phoning home after lights-out, and letting fly words describing bodily functions during Sunday morning services. If they could have figured out how, the administrators would have made daydreaming contraband, too.

I made a little signal, drawing my hands around my neck and becoming my own noose, but Todd just frowned and went about the business of packing another bowl.

"Put in a tape, Beaner," he said.

I slammed the drawer on my colored highlighter pens and flipped through the collection of tapes on my bookshelf. At this point in my tenure at Stillwater, I had eighty-seven Grateful Dead bootlegs in all, the most of anybody except for Skippy down the hall with the bitching stereo system. Skippy had about four more. I kept my collection arranged according to date. If the tape had a *B* on the label, that meant it was bogus. If it was a ripping tape, then I put an *R* on it. If it was a really ripping tape, then I put an *R* with a star or two next to it. I had three ripping-star tapes and a couple of two-stars. What I wanted was an *R* with three stars. That's what every real Dead Head wanted—a ripping, kick-ass three-star tape. The Grateful Dead calendar tacked to the corkboard above my desk indicated that Freedom Coliseum was next up on the tour schedule—small arena, intimate space, the perfect venue for seizing my version of the Holy Grail and making up for all my woes.

"What is this shit?" Captain Puckwhacker leaned across the metal frame of the bed after I had plugged in Foxboro '89. We were treated to about twenty straight seconds of squelch before crowd noise kicked in. The light from the counter on the tape deck illuminated the dude's face from the bottom up, and for a second I couldn't tell his chin from his forehead. The fluorescent lights in all the rooms at Stillwater made everyone look like they were suffering from some strange disease or, worse, like they had dropped in from another planet and were about to perform physical examinations.

"Jerry," I explained.

The sound of feedback triggered a thousand happy synapses and made it easier to take the hit of the dope Todd passed my way. While I puffed, the tape rolled past the hissing and popping and screeching into something that began to sound like music. Todd eased back onto his bed and smiled a Cheshire cat smile, the kind of smile he gets when the smoke session he is presiding over is about to dip into an interesting phase. The Captain took the hookah I passed to him, sucked down his second hit, and coughed and coughed until Todd and I figured he was about to cough up a lung. The dope in the bowl glowed, and a wisp of smoke curled toward the ceiling, gyrating its way into the atmosphere, another parade of dancing bears making its way toward heaven, another bit of intellectual matter up in smoke.

"My thing is pure, dude," I explained.

Captain Puckwhacker hacked a few more times and held his chest.

"We just bet," he said in a way that made me know for sure he and I were not going to become pals anytime soon. I was waiting for him to make a crack about my mother, but the guy surprised me and handed back the hookah.

In the conversational gap that followed, a small strand of sunlight shimmered across the floor and lit up the room like the upside-down words of God in one of those Dutch paintings we had to look at in art history class. Like most people, I was more relaxed when I didn't have to figure out what the crazy prophecy breaking out at my feet was—a sign to join a seminary, stop eating meat, pick up the dirty clothes in my closet. The list of what I needed to change burst through my head like a comet rounding a dark galaxy: My geometry grade was a little on the low side, my GPA sucked, I wanted to give my stepfather a call, and the Freedom show was on the horizon, promising a bootleg as juicy as fruit on a tree, ready to be plucked. Captain P. settled back away from the light, and the three of us began to have one of those conversations stoned people have when there are no *Star Trek* reruns on to keep them occupied.

"Do you ever wonder what it would be like to know the future?" the Captain asked.

"No," Todd and I said together.

"You never once thought about what it would be like to ride around in spaceships and do green space babes?"

"The spaceships," I said, trying to change the subject

from what would inevitably lead to a discussion of my mother.

"Screw the future," Todd said. "That's not what it's going to look like."

But before Todd could lay some wisdom on us about what the world would be like in the next millennium—little handheld phones that took pictures, cars that ran on batteries—someone knocked on the door—four steady bangs, our code—and I got up to let in Kenny J. He staggered across my dirty laundry and plopped himself down on my bed, his fly gaping open under his untucked shirt. His face didn't hold much in the way of expression, just looked like someone had stolen it. There was nothing—not age, fear, or loathing—that could make Kenny J. change his squint, the bad-attitude lock on his jaw. He might have been a granite wall or a blank sheet of paper in another life for all I could gauge his reaction to us hanging out, getting high with James Tiberius Puckwhacker. Guys like Kenny J. I imagined becoming prison wardens someday, though Kenny, in all likelihood, was going to follow in his father's footsteps and become a stockbroker. Our room seemed to close down with the four of us sitting in it, the light trickling away again behind the window, the building rustling with the loose energy of too many people with too much time on their hands.

The tape in the deck cut out, and I could hear Kenny J. breathing through his nose and Haley the goldfish bumping against his bowl underneath my bed. Haley was a pretty obese goldfish, one of those pets traded around in the dorm from one guy to another and then finally traded to Todd to pay back a debt. Todd was considerate about allowing Haley to become more my goldfish than his. Over time Haley had bonded with me. I took him out every couple of days, brushed the dust off his bowl, showed him the light of day, and fed him seeds from Todd's pot stash along with his pellets, hoping to cheer him up. Haley spent his days negotiating his way around and around the one piece of plastic seaweed that decorated his bowl. Around and around. I suppose it wasn't too bad a life for a fish. At least he was loved.

In those few seconds of soft bumping and breathing, I forgot about the fading light of the afternoon, and that I was sitting among friends and a three-goal-a-game scorer BMOC who might have been a narc. Our dorm was the farthest out of the four dorms on the Stillwater campus, farther out than the row of faculty housing, the

18

chapel, two classroom buildings, the ice rink, the horse barn, the shooting range, and the golf course. Another mile cut the school off from the town of Stillwater, the plastic Santas and Christmas lights, the blue-plate specials and dollar-a-head bingo nights. From our window, where the bull's-eye tapestry was pulled aside, we could see the carpet of trees separating the school from Route 8 and the rest of Connecticut to the east and New York State to the west. Since we had begun our smoke session, the clouds had packed together in an effort to snow. The wind had died. The sun had dropped another foot into the horizon. Beyond Connecticut, the hills rolled over each other and finally got serious toward the Adirondacks and lower Appalachians, cornering all of us preppies in the north and east, forcing us together and the rest of the world out.

Unlike most boarding schools in Connecticut, Stillwater wasn't built in one of those perfect little towns with ordinances prohibiting people from using old tires as planters and building mailboxes to look like chicken coops. Stillwater the town was a pretty hideous-looking place. In 1955, a flood wiped out half the buildings and left a few factories, an old drive-in movie theater,

Stillwater Academy on the hill, and a junior high school. Anything that might have had some quality or historical value was destroyed immediately, and most of the buildings were not rebuilt until the 1970s, when plywood and aluminum siding were making an appearance. Even the fall leaves in Stillwater weren't too scenic, since they got soggy and fell off in early October every year. If anything, Stillwater was the perfect place to build a penitentiary, a sewage treatment plant, or a toaster factory, not a school.

"They ought to deep-six *Deep Space Nine*," Kenny J. said, breaking the silence that had stuffed itself into our dark little room.

"Hear, hear," Todd seconded.

"We think the chick with freckles has nice tits," the hockey player said.

Kenny J. pulled a red ball out of his pocket, one of his favorite, slightly moronic things to do. The ball came from a paddle game and had a staple on it where the rubber string used to be. Kenny had a room full of old toys like the paddle game, which had broken a long time ago and which he transported around school with him for special occasions. Because I hadn't expected it, and because the bong hits had flustered the rat that turns the wheel inside my head, I laughed. The ball could have been a clown nose, and (probably because I was stoned) for a second I thought it *was* a clown nose. Suddenly I knew why clown noses were funny. Before that moment, I had thought they were stupid. Kenny J. kept himself from smiling at his own joke and patted his pants. He discovered his unzipped fly, pulled on it, but had no luck.

"Do that again," I begged, meaning the ball and not the patting and rezipping of his pants.

Captain Puckwhacker smirked, and Kenny J. pulled the ball back out of his pocket. The ball squeaked another round of ha-ha out of us. After that we tried to go back to having a conversation. Todd convinced the Captain to buy an eighth and whipped out the scale again. I tried to defend that one *Deep Space Nine* character that slept in a bucket, but the words stuck in a dry spot between my brain and my throat, and I only got about half of what I was trying to say out. Captain Puckwhacker wasn't doing much better. He pulled on the edge of his sweater sleeve, spent ten minutes trying to get one thread that had come loose to tear off. He finally leaned over and bit it. Kenny J. pulled the red ball out of his pocket a third time and held it. The red ball made me so happy I just about burst.

"Idiotic." Captain P. spit the thread from his teeth.

"Give me that," I demanded, but Kenny put the ball back in his pocket and pretended it wasn't there.

Then Todd went into one of his spiels. Even stoned, Todd can talk on any subject with more confidence than anyone I've ever met. I don't know how the guy does it, since dope in my system usually means words have to be turned over a few times before they'll rev up. In any case, Todd went into one of his long speeches about the comparative disadvantages of Klingon physiology in battle situations. Captain P. did the best he could to get his purchase into a Ziploc before Todd appropriated some of it for a fat one he was rolling up, working while he talked, demonstrating how the larger forehead size of Klingons meant more brains but made their heads harder to lug around. He pointed out that the foreheads were still getting bigger, adding at least twenty pounds to their size since the old *Star Trek*. I followed most of what Todd was saying, but to tell you the truth, I'd heard it before. It might even have been my idea once, or Kenny J.'s. Todd's not above stealing when he's wasted. He makes everything sound better, though, and that's his justification.

"It proves the theory of evolution," he said, which is what I had said, or what Kenny J. had said, a long time ago.

"Interesting." The Captain offered his approval.

Kenny J. pulled the ball back out of his pocket a fourth time, and I wondered how many times he could play the same trick. I made him pull it out a few more times, in and then out, like a kid playing peekaboo. While Captain Puckwhacker tried to argue with Todd about the shake he had weighed into the dope, the ball got so funny that I couldn't look at it anymore. I didn't want to know that something could be so beautiful, so magical, and not really be anything at all. Some people say that drugs are a shortcut to enlightenment, but I don't buy that. There were enough surprises edging their way into the afternoon that I knew there had to be a miracle on the way. I'm not saying I was looking forward to world peace breaking out, my history grade taking a flying leap out of the D range, a sudden achievement of normalcy in the parental arena, or even a three-star bootleg to be delivered unto me before the weekend was out. I was just unaccountably happy watching a little red ball pop out of somebody's pocket.

If I could have stopped time, I might have stopped it there and hovered like Kenny's red clown ball in mid-air, like the guy on the Saratoga tape who flies and falls with every listening. As it was, deviant karma was bound to come raining down on my rich and privileged life, scattering the ducks of fortune that had been aligned by some anonymous God in my honor, and Aetna Life & Casualty in Hartford never did make an umbrella for that. After Stillwater, most guys I knew planned to go to big-money colleges and then—after their drug habits had been overcome—to cash in on their parents' alumni status to get themselves into Princeton or Dartmouth for their MBA or law degrees. Up until then, I had kind of banked on the same fate myself, and who could blame me for staying caught in the traditional cycle of greed and more greed? The Captain propped himself up on the bed and let the string from his sweater slide out from between his teeth.

"So do you think you could introduce us to your mother this weekend?" he asked. To tell you the truth, I'm surprised I didn't see the question coming.

LOOKS LIKE RAIN

CAPTAIN PUCKWHACKER IGNORED his own joke and suddenly began jabbering about Parents' Weekend, telling us about his girlfriend's upcoming visit, describing what a great lay she was, the little things she did in the sack, piling on the hockey player flourishes and not holding back on the physical gestures. He started out talking normally but got louder in order to convince us of the parts that were obviously bullshit. It all meant more in his language than in ours, and I wouldn't have paid attention at all, what with the dope having settled me into a state just this side of comatose and his reference to my mother still ticking me off, but before the sex talk, I had been thinking about the chances of pulling down my ideal tape. I sat up from where I had built a small nest in my dirty clothes, a complication worming its way into the happy garden of my mood.

"Parents' Weekend is next weekend, dude," I said, and straight off, Todd, Captain Puckwhacker, and Kenny J. unanimously corrected me. I had been so messed up over the previous few days that I had not noticed that Parents' Weekend had officially begun, that the grounds crew was already on a mad crusade to fluff up the ornamental shrubbery, and that the faculty had beaten all the dust out of their erasers.

Important information had been sneaking up on me all fall, perhaps a warning that Todd's Thai stick had begun to make my gears turn slower or that my mother's antics had eaten through what had never been my model boy facade and attacked my organizational skills. Todd's parents had given him a full reprieve from the handshaking and check signing that the headmaster put the rest of us through. Kenny J.'s parents were coming, but Kenny had convinced them to score some tickets and sign him out for the trip to Freedom rather than force him to attend the festivities. Kenny's family was as weird as Kenny and they indulged his idiosyncrasies when they visited, slipped money into the breast pocket of his jacket, let him smoke cigars and drink wine when they took him out to dinner. Kenny J. had even brought his mother to our room once to smoke dope, a tightly packed jay that she inhaled while standing and held in the tips of her lacquered fingers, the same deadpan expression on her face that Kenny puffed with.

I'd been trying for the last few days to get through to my mother, leaving messages with her agent, with Vonda, the housekeeper, and even at my stepfather's office, but she hadn't returned my calls, maybe because she was caught up in her book tour or her photo shoot, but more likely because she was avoiding me for a while, giving me time to come around after our last phone conversation, when I had gone slightly ballistic. If my mother was going to visit for Parents' Weekend, as she had mentioned she might back in September, when she typically made promises about care packages and teddy bears as a way of getting me out the door, then I needed to be ready for our conversation to continue and for me to hear her side one more time. I had heard that mothers sometimes helped their sons clean their rooms, and that seemed like a safe, private outlet for our time together. On the other hand, I also knew several dozen guys who would have wanted her to make their beds, too, or who would have liked to be on hand to watch her make mine. I glanced over at the Captain, who seemed to be waiting for what I was going to say about her.

"A relative of mine might be showing up for a few minutes" is all I said, but sadly that's all it took.

Kenny J., Todd, and Captain P. all looked at me, and the bong momentarily halted its progression. Todd did me the kindness of saying, "Going to Freedom without the Little Freak will be like Batman cape-crusading without Robin or Captain Picard boldly going without Number One"—although my failure to get the dates straight made me wonder why some guys have sidekicks, since they'd be a lot more invulnerable without them, what with Robin spending half his time tied to a rotating saw and Number One being a big fat pain in the ass. Sidekicks are almost as dangerous to superheroes as Kryptonite is to Superman. While I tried to read what was in Todd's face—desire to sneak a peek at my mother or determination to make it to Freedom to deepen his groovy—he chose another tape, New Haven 1988. Not a bad selection, though the crowd noise overpowers the sound of the tunes, and there's a lot of hissing and popping.

Captain Puckwhacker held up his bag of dope and looked it over, a tactic I recognized as playing innocent in order to get information out of me slowly. "Man, this is good shit. We like this shit."

"Don't call it 'shit,' dude," I said.

"No," Kenny J. confirmed.

The Captain must have heard someone call dope "shit" in the movies and thought it was the correct thing to say when breaking bread with guys like us. Nobody else I knew called dope "shit"—freaks especially had more respect. The movies are bad for the image of dope smokers. They make us look like burned-out idiots who drop the words *cool* and *man* into every other sentence, but there's more to us than that. In a lot of cases, we're normal-looking, might even go yachting with our parents every once in a while or for a ride in a BMW. I had even known some freaks who were just as normal-looking as the Captain, or the headmaster, just not as uptight. Things like love beads and Birkenstocks are only part of our image, not the whole package. The whole image is deeper than the word *shit*.

"Have some respect, dude," I instructed him.

"Steve," Captain Puckwhacker said.

"Steve?" I repeated. I didn't know what the hell he was talking about.

"Poltergeist," Kenny J. explained, holding up and pointing at the hookah.

"Steve," the hockey player said again, thumping the blue wool at the center of his chest. "Not 'dude.' Not 'man.' Steve."

I hate to say it, but the guy looked like a Steve or a Kent or a Pete now that I had been forced to really take him in. At Stillwater, hockey players seemed to have names like labels. If a guy had a name like Pete or Kevin, he most likely got into Stillwater on an athletic scholarship. If he had a name like Gordie, you could be 90 percent sure he played defense—unless he was Canadian, I guess. In that case, there was no telling. Normally I wouldn't have tried talking to a Steve—it was a good way to find myself beaten up, head-flushed, or towel-whipped in the shower room. The reason I hadn't already fallen victim to his evil all-American-ness was a testament to the quality of the day, the high number of weird vibes in the air, and the likelihood that the guy was so stoned he might have been having problems communicating with his mother ship.

"Steve?" I said again.

"You heard me," Captain Steven "Steve" Puckwhacker said, only with all the dope he had smoked melting his mouth and my eardrums, it sounded like "Ewe herb me" or "U nerd me," some kind of foreign language for Ken dolls.

He went back to his sweater, pulling on the loose thread in the cuff, flossing his teeth with it. The guy didn't have an ultrabright smile for nothing. I offered him my hand, and after only a second of thinking better of it, maybe in order to emphasize the universal truth of his "Steve-ness," he let go of his sweater and took it, latched on to it with one of those firm grips that involved invasive eye contact and made me drop pencils for a week. I didn't think he had it in him to be decent, but all kinds of things can lurk in a guy. He finished shaking and retreated to the corner of my bed, leaning his head up against the tapestry on the wall and rubbing the smoke out of his eyes. Todd banged on his knee, picking up some of the "Terrapin Station" groove coming out of the tape deck.

"Since you're skipping without the Little Freakster"— Kenny J. addressed Todd, thumping along too, his elbows going at considerable angles to his body and in no way resembling the beat laid down by the music—"join the family. We're all going."

Todd reached out from his bed to pick up the hookah. I could tell he was considering the invitation, deciding whether he would be losing out on a prime business opportunity at the Freedom show by staying and calculating what the long-term dividends might be of going with the James family. Before firing up the bowl, he loosened his tie. His jacket was still on and his shoes were lined up next to his desk. He seemed to be sizing up Kenny, considering his sidekick potential and measuring him for his metaphorical cape. He had the advantage of having a lot to offer any guy with a trust fund who was looking for someone more hip to clue him in. Sometimes he failed to appreciate the work, the stress, that went into being his chief underling. If it had been me who had received the postcard (and in my case it would have been a Post-it on the back of an allowance check), I would have hung around the campus waiting for him, or for my mother, or for whoever bounded into my life, willing to play hero to my pitiful half of a dynamic duo.

"Which brings me to our reason for being here," Steve said.

"More dope?" Todd asked, the salesman in him coming to full attention.

"The Freakster's mother," Steve said.

The statement seemed to satisfy him. I could tell his favorite part of being a hockey player, aside from the obvious thrill of whacking pucks into a net, was getting to rain bullshit on guys like me, guys who were so low down on the totem pole that we had few inferiors. My two choices in the face of such backhanded friendliness had always been either to get uptight and find myself hung out on a flagpole by my underpants or do the humiliating to myself in order to create a diversion. To an outsider, the two things might have seemed equal: flagpoles or having to eat eight butter pats for dinner, but the first required expressing public anger about my private life. My emotions regarding my mother were public enough. I was by nature a guy who liked to keep things peaceful. Hanging with Kenny J. and letting my fly gape open, too, was sort of like a Buddhist monk slipping into his mantra.

Being the life of the party worked, but I still had to

be conscious of what could trip me up and either bury it or gloss it over with some kind of silliness or a dash of smart-ass. I had already figured out that Steve didn't know yet about the *Playboy* spread or else his cork would have popped before the third bong hit, testosterone being a tough thing to control. Yet I had hours and hours more of pain to negotiate. I had years and years of history to bury.

Back when I was an unsuspecting, innocent three-year-old, for example, my mother had posed for *Esquire*. She hadn't yet hit the bestseller list, and it looked like a good way to advertise her first book. The photo the magazine used was of her in the shower, and they airbrushed just enough of her to give her a Venus-on-the-half-shell look, a way of making the thing more artistic and her more like the goddess of love she was attempting to be. I was in the foreground of some of the proofs, pink and angry, my mouth wide open and my wrists bent up like I was trying to fly. I remember wondering what the hell sixteen people were doing in our bathroom shining bright lights in our direction, and I remember one fat guy calling the shots and telling me to calm down. I was also stark naked, and let me just say that at three I didn't have much worth showing off.

There was also my mother's appearance on *Bunny Bellwether* in September. The usual hockey players and entertainment committee members were on hand in the proctor's suite to witness that humiliation. My mother looked even more of a knockout than usual and everyone responded, even with the terrible reception on the proctor's set. The topic on the *Bunny* show was "Parents of Teenage Homosexuals." The camera panned over to my mom, lingering on her low neckline, and then it panned back to a parent. A caption that said "Parent of a Homosexual" appeared on the screen underneath a parent's face. Then the camera cut to a kid, and a caption that said "Homosexual" appeared.

"Do you have any advice for these mothers?" Bunny asked my mother, referring to the row of miserable-looking guests on the stage—fat thirtysomething women, one opinionated, hatchet-faced husband in a checked shirt, and a half dozen sulking and squirming children in pegged pants and Doc Martens sliding down into their leather-backed chairs.

The thing was that these were "real people" as opposed to the righteous fabric-softener-buying middle-

American portion of Bunny's audience—the Hitler Authoritarian Judgmentalists. A lot of Stillwaterites were hooked on watching cop and rescue dramas, Court TV, and talk shows just so they could get a glimpse of "real people"—people not like them. The television jumped and hissed and one of the hockey players got up and slapped the side to get rid of the vertical quivering in the middle. My mother seemed to feel the jolt as she considered Bunny's question. Then she crossed her legs and ran her hand down her thigh to pull her skirt down (a big disappointment to the Stillwater portion of her viewing audience, let me tell you). "Normal child rearing," my mother said, "is a delicate thing. We can't ever really know the best way to educate our children about their sexual identity. We can only learn to accept them for who they are."

Bunny nodded, folded her arms, and tucked her microphone under her elbow. Whereas the guys in the proctor's apartment latched on to the "healthy sexual identity" part of my mother's answer, I began to worry about what might come next. I wondered if Bunny knew that my mother had no business giving advice on adolescents, had made a mess of her own life and wasn't doing too well with normal child rearing either. My mother didn't seem worried about Bunny's folded arms. "I have a son, too," my mother said, trying to appease one of the sadder-looking women. She didn't elaborate on my identity (sexual or otherwise). The guys in the room started laughing. One of them, a guy I recognized from my Latin class, turned and looked at me hanging out by the door.

"Hey, dude," I greeted him, wishing he would go to hell.

"Did you just call me 'dude'?" he asked.

"Dude" is a term of camaraderie among fellow Jerry-ites, a way of extending friendship without straining the brain cells trying to remember a name. The guy gave me one of those looks that people give you when they're pissed off at you for no reason. He pushed his hair off his forehead and raised his voice so that the other guys could hear him over the television set.

"Homo," he said, loudly enough that a couple of guys tossing a lacrosse ball back and forth in the hall overheard the joke and came in for a look-see.

It was pretty clear that the guy actually thought I was the kind of guy who got off doing other guys, and though I knew he suffered pain in his homophobic insecurity, his tone ticked me off. I was still a virgin—that rumor had gotten around thanks to Todd, who found out when my mother mentioned it once on TV. Todd and my mother both maintained the theory that it was better to have bad news out in the open, although it was more frequently my bad news than theirs that got spread. And to tell you the truth, I was a little uncomfortably comfortable with my lack of experience. Although I wasn't a faggot, I must have had some faggot years in there, which accounted for the awkwardness I felt every time somebody raised the subject. I wasn't sure enough of what it felt like to be a faggot, though, to come up with much of an answer every time the question got raised.

"Ha-ha," I tried. "That's a good one."

In addition to being potentially sexually confused, I was given to "occasional lapses into violence as a direct reaction to shame," according to my mother and Dr. Keller, the school psychologist. I had been referred to Dr. Keller the year before, when the dope smoking kicked in and my grades tanked. Dr. K and I spent one happy afternoon together every week and watched each other's hair grow. But in Latin class, I still had to fight an urge to scream at the top of my lungs and pull my pants down. It wasn't the *"amo, amas, amat"* that drove me nuts. It was the dead-language thing, learning words that would never help me talk to anybody. I never meant to be the confused fuckup that I so obviously was. I had the thinnest skin on the planet. My mother said it had something to do with the size of my pores, how much stuff seemed to seep into me, how overstimulated I got any time anyone gave me a lollipop as a kid or I patted a dog or something. Dr. Keller could have diagnosed me as having a problem with controlled substances, but my real addiction was to my fellow human beings. I couldn't stop giving a damn about what they thought of me.

A perfect freak would have handled the situation differently. A totally committed freak would have been friendly to the guy with the homophobia, reminded himself that we were all Jerry's kids for a reason. Sometimes I thought about my Jerryism and how I tended to get on the deficit side when I didn't mean to. Fortunately, Jerry wasn't one of those guys, like Buddha or Christ or Deepak, that you had to be worthy of to worship. Otherwise there would have been no tape collection, no tie-dye, no "Dark Star." Stillwater was a tough place to keep Jerryism in practice. Peace and love didn't pour out of the air vents; in fact, it was more like the opposite. A guy had to fight off Authoritarian Bullshit from the first breath he took in the morning until he went to bed at night. No telling what kind of trouble a real homosexual would have gotten into at Stillwater, as hard as it was on the fringes.

When my mother called me on the phone not long after the *Bunny* show to tell me about the centerfold, we calmly discussed the nature of the thing, how much weight she planned to lose, just exactly what pose she had agreed to have shot. She was nervous as hell, and I could tell from her voice over the line that she had some misgivings. A skinny freshman kid waited in the hallway near the booth. I pulled the receiver tight toward my ear and tried to stare him down. He looked at his fingernails and at the clock in the hallway, but I knew what he was up to. At the end of the hall, I could hear the beginning music from some television show coming out of the proctor's apartment.

"Mom," I said into the phone.

"I was just thinking," she said.

"Mom, people I know are going to see this . . . " I tried to explain my side of the issue.

The guy in the hallway smirked and turned his back, acting like he had to get closer to the booth to pick up a book. My mother and I went back and forth and I pictured her up in her room, sitting against her chintz pillowcases, the light of her laptop illuminating her face. She accused me of being a stick-in-the-mud, a fuddy-duddy, the same thing she had called my stepfather in their fights over the summer, and I knew that I was being uptight, maybe selfish. On the other hand, if your mother writes books about oral and anal sex, then your role in an all-male boarding school requires you to do some fighting back. Shit, most of the guys I knew were so in love with my mother they'd beat off to her book jacket photos, and this list of wannabe lovers didn't just include Steve; it included my roommate, my best friends, and my English and math instructors. The sad thing was that getting to see her nude wasn't going to be any worse than what they'd all done in their imaginations for the last two and a half years. And since I had imagined them all imagining, I had an oedipal complex going with the whole damn world. Try to beat *that* for psycho-Freudian trauma.

Sometimes I didn't want to be the person I was,

feeling the things I was feeling. I loved my mother, but not precisely in the same way the rest of the world seemed to love her, and definitely not in the same way Steve and his buddies showed their affection. There were two of her, one who was happy and could make anything funny, even a fight with my stepfather, and another who got restless and shifted me off on Vonda, or to some damn camp or school. Lately I was backing my stepfather in the fights he and she were having and wanting him to win so that she would become less self-interested, more of a team player, more the kind of mother who would show up for Parents' Weekend to help me fold my clothes and not strip for a magazine with a subscription list in the millions.

Maybe my mother could rain enough good times on me to get me through another round of divorce, but my stepfather Knees, for the time he lingered on the scene, gave me a taste of what it might have been like to live in a happy television family, one where getaway divorces weren't always so necessary. He did things like tousle my hair on the way out the door to catch his train. Even in the privacy of her own home, in her unairbrushed state, my mother had quirks that took some getting used to:

bad breath in the morning, a preference for sleeping with her dog, Rufus, and a hell of an insecurity about what people thought of her, so much so that she annoyed the heck out of me at more than one breakfast when I was just trying to eat my eggs.

As Todd, Steve, Kenny J., and I sat in our room with the bong making its listless rounds, the three of them discussed her publicized points while I closed my eyes and tried to sink a little deeper into the tune on the tape deck—"Truckin'"—just what I wanted to do. If my mother showed up at Stillwater for Parents' Weekend, she'd want to talk about her photo shoot while we sat over our turkey, the goddamned headmaster to our right and the proctor on the left, all ears trained on us. She doesn't believe in privacy, or in relationships where mothers don't tell their sons that they think their right nipple might need lifting. I didn't need just to get past the holidays to feel safe again. I needed to fast-forward into the next century.

BOX OF RAIN

BACK IN THE STONE AGE, my stepfather Knees had been a Stillwaterite, too, and because he had retained the nickname one of his old-fart classmates had bestowed on him, I assumed that he had enjoyed the experience. Either that or time had worked its amnesia. I'd seen the same thing in old dudes on programs I'd caught on PBS. There they would be, sitting in stuffed chairs, books behind them, talking lovingly about their time in some war or how they ate potato peels during the Depression. While he was a sophomore at Stillwater, Knees had broken a school track record and his real name, Kennebec Douglas, was on a wall in the gym. His classmates might have dubbed him Knees because he had churned up some dirt or because he had this habit of running his hands down the front of his pants when he sat, like some kind of school psychologist or deep-thinking professor type. Or I guess there could even have been some "homo" inside joke having to do with patellas I wasn't up on, some kind of lingo from the fifties that Knees carried around with him like a sad truth.

No other stepfather had ever made his kind of an impression. Usually changes in the state of my hyphenation happened quickly and I found out three or four weeks after the fact, via a Post-it note stuck to an allowance check or some damn thing like that. A person would have had to know Knees to see the subtle difference between him and a half million other guys from Westchester and Greenwich counties. He walked the dog after seven every evening, went soft around the eyes when he talked about the stock exchange, and had married my mother in a fit of midlife doubt, attracted to her light the way brown moths hover around a lamp on a long summer evening. He was a handshaker like the husbands who had preceded him, yet there was something different about his grip. His hand was warmer, cool where his wedding ring passed over the fourth finger on his left hand but dry around the palms. He didn't have one of those clammy death-hold affairs that a suit-to-be had to practice at places like Stillwater and strengthen over a lifetime.

Only a year and a half earlier, I had met Knees for the first time at Cafe Un Deux Trois in downtown New York City. Todd had been with me and we found Knees sitting in a booth by himself in the corner waiting for us. Before we got a chance to introduce ourselves, Knees' palm shot out and grabbed Todd's, welcoming him to his family. He didn't seem to see me at first, standing directly behind Todd in a skirt and a couple of silver bangles, but I have to say he didn't react badly when we finally set him straight about who was who. A lot of Dead Head guys were wearing skirts that spring—they're comfortable in hot weather. I usually put on some kind of show for my new stepfathers as a way of making sure they knew what they were getting into.

He made more or less the same speech he had made to Todd a few seconds earlier, and, to my surprise, it came off sounding sincere. In the months that followed, when he caught me home from school on vacation or back from the sailing camp, he asked me questions about my favorite baseball team and my roommate situation. He turned out to be a killer croquet player, and I've got memories of him on the lawn after dark in the summer, whacking the final post with his ball and doing a little victory dance in the glow of the bug zapper on the porch.

Unlike my other stepfathers, when Knees made a lousy shot, he didn't blame it on the unevenness of the grounds or the gnats swarming around his head. He didn't steer around his emotions, either. He explained to me that having a new wife and stepson was quite a pleasure. When he was confused, he looked confused. When he was thoughtful, he ran his hands down the front of his pants or checked his watch. I answered his questions about baseball by trotting out the few facts I had on Shaquille O'Neal and he didn't stop me even though I could tell he knew I was bullshitting.

Somehow he got word that my mom and I had sparred on the phone. Knees showed up at Stillwater and convinced somebody in the headmaster's office to call me out of Latin class. Right away, I became suspicious, since step-units don't usually interrupt their step-tax-deductions' academic advancement unless they've got something ugly on their minds to discuss. He complimented me on my tie, and since guys with ties don't need encouraging, I expected him to tell me that he was having trouble with my mother and that their marriage might be over. I even expected him to tell me exactly what he ended up telling me, that he was moving back to his apartment in the city before the holidays. What I hadn't prepared myself for, though, at least emotionally, was to care.

When I met him at the proctor's apartment, he asked me if I wanted to have lunch with him and I said yes. We didn't go far, just to Sam's lunch counter down the street, one of those places that mostly caters to fat guys who wear their wallets chained to their belt loops. I rode in the front seat of his Beamer, taking in the scenery and listening to the Mozart that he had plugged into the deck. The high notes, the flute, and the piano floated like boats and got me in the heart the way Jerry got me. A purist would have said that there was no comparison, but I could engage in Mozart if I had to be Jerry-less, add my own lyrics in the parts that seemed dry, and let my mind drift on the current. Usually Todd invited himself along on my family outings to get himself out of school, but this time he had a deal going down with a couple of lower-tier freaks looking for an eighth to keep them groovy. It was just Knees and me, not really trying to speak to each other at first, just sort of staring off into our private space.

It was too bad that Sam's was the only place I could think of for us to go to lunch. If I had been thinking at all, I would have talked Knees into taking me to Hu Fong's so I could down a couple of mai tais. Instead, we took the last two swivel stools at the counter at Sam's, in front of an open porthole with an aging guy in a paper hat standing behind it, most likely Sam himself, long past retirement age. He was busy frying up burgers, flipping and scraping his way through the lunch rush. Without even looking at us, Sam hobbled out from behind his partition, slapped down a couple of paper napkins, two sweaty glasses of water, and some bent silverware. After pouring himself a Coke, he went back through the swinging door and flipped some more burgers. I pulled a plastic menu from the ring holder by our place mats and turned the pages back and forth, looking for what I thought I might want to eat. A lot of the choices were right there on the menu—I mean, physically sticking to it.

"What'll you have?" A waitress who sensed there was something big going down between Knees and me ignored a row of empty coffee cups and hurried to get to us. She poured coffee into Knees' mug, taking her time, hovering over us in case we said something she might find interesting.

"I'll have a Reuben," Knees said, folding his plastic menu closed and handing it to her. She took a pencil out from behind her ear and wrote the order down.

"I'll have a hot dog," I said.

Knees checked his Rolex. I'd seen the gesture before. A flash of light reflected across the ceiling as his forearm rotated toward his chest and the watch face caught the sun coming through the partially washed windows. We were surrounded by a group of middle-aged men having a conversation about PVC tubing. Taken in by the reflection, they looked up and then back down again at their plates as if they had just had a group hallucination. Sam's gets some of the local business crowd, but mostly it gets the kinds of customers you never see anyplace else except at lunch counters. A group of fat men in a booth near us smoked cigars and held their coffee cups up for a refill. Down the counter from us, a woman conversed with her glass of grapefruit juice. Before either Knees or I had said a single thing to the other, the waitress arrived with the Reuben and the hot dog. My stepfather got about midway through the Reuben before he swiveled on his stool to face me.

"Son," he said—his name for me.

"Yes?" I answered.

This was all he had gotten around to since we had climbed out of the car. Even the waitress had lost interest and was at the other side of the counter.

"Have you ever considered a career in the legal field?" he asked me, the emotional stuff getting into his voice.

"Legal career?" I asked.

"Yes." He picked a piece of sauerkraut out of his Reuben and put it on the edge of his plate.

"No," I said.

Finally he put the Reuben down altogether. "You know I love you and your mother very much . . ." he began.

I found myself listening to him, not so much to what he was saying exactly but to the way in which he was saying it. He talked about responsibility. He described a roommate he had back in the day who had given him some trouble, the kind of stuff that would get a dude a nickname if they said it in the dorm. I noticed that he had to rub his hands against his pants and check his watch, the nervous gestures coming more rapidly now. The juice from the sauerkraut formed a puddle on his plate, and he took the time to sop it up with a napkin.

How could I tell the guy to stop? That it didn't exactly matter? That he was feeling sorry for me while I had been through the situation enough times before to handle it on my own. If enough crazy things happen to you in your life, you get to thinking of some of them as funny when they happen to you again. That's what it felt like, sitting across from him, like he was telling me some great big joke that was funnier than hell, only he was telling it like it was the sermon of a lifetime. His throat clicked as he paused for me to say something, but he knew just as well as I did that there was nothing left to be said. The waitress sensed that she had missed her moment and refilled coffee cups down the line, hustling her way back to us as fast as she could. I didn't wait for her to close in before tilting my hot dog in my stepfather's direction.

"Well, here's looking at you," I said.

Lame, I know. It didn't feel right, but at least the waitress hadn't overheard and discovered how big an ass I was. The truth was I appreciated the sensei stuff and I wondered what it would be like to lean over into his lap and bawl my eyes out, a combination of things putting pressure on me, I guess: sorrow that I wasn't going to see him again and self-pity for my own lonelier state. I felt like I was seeing just how good a father could be. Sure, I'd had my dreams about fathers when I was a small kid, but they were buried by the time I had met Knees, a thing of the past—or at least *I* had thought so.

I could have been one of those guys who had a great family—happy parents, a little sister who looked just like me—but, hell, that just wasn't what I'd been dealt. I could have been a guy like the hall monitor on our floor—with no friends, really, who had to whine his way into people's rooms and then betray them to the administration to get any respect—but, instead, I was me, a guy cursed by his relationships to other people, who carried the weight of my mom's shortcomings and pretended not to care. When the door to our dorm room opened and woke me from my doze and the staircase of memories I had fallen down, my stepfather glinted in my consciousness like the reflection of his watch, here and then gone. I was back with Todd and Walt, and the two painful months of being without Knees swelled and faded.

It took me a minute to figure out where I was and what

I was doing with drool on my face and who was marching across my laundry to sit down on my bed. The number of hockey players in our room quadrupled—numbers 46, 27, and 8 all making themselves comfortable next to Steve. At first, I thought my vision had become impaired on account of my drowsiness, but then their laughter sucked the air right out from between the walls, and I knew they were no illusion. Apparently one of the hockey players had farted, and it was bringing the house down all around. In my opinion, farting is only funny sometimes. Everyone in a room after a fart gets the joke except the farter himself. I always feel stupid and alone when I fart, especially when I might have tried to slip it in unnoticed. It takes a certain kind of insensitivity to wish that kind of discomfort on somebody else. For hockey players, though, farting is a brotherhood ritual, part of their existential way of expressing themselves.

"We think you should set us up," Steve said, noticing that I was back among them.

"Who?" the hockey players asked.

"The Freakster's mother. She's coming for Parents' Weekend," Steve explained.

Todd looked at Kenny J., and Kenny J. looked at his

fingernails. The hockey players did one of their high-five cheers.

"C'mon," Steve practically whined.

"Anybody in the mood to catch *Jeopardy!*?" I asked.

"No," the hockey players answered in chorus.

"Stupid questions for one thousand, Alex." Kenny J. stretched out on the floor.

"Don't be so melodramatic, Beaner," Todd said.

The one and only time my mother had ever set foot on the Stillwater campus was the day she dropped me off that year and left me standing on the drive with a teddy bear. She has always had the mistaken impression that I'm the kind of guy who likes teddy bears. I get them for Christmas, birthdays, and any other holiday that occurs to her. Have you ever tossed a teddy bear in the garbage? The way its black button eyes stare up at you, it's frightening. In a million years, I wasn't going to admit that I didn't know what the hell my mother was going to do for Parents' Weekend, that I never knew what my mother was going to do. She might show up, but then again, Santa Claus might also be real and the tooth fairy is my best chick friend.

"Hey, can we come to your house for Christmas?"

Steve suddenly got even funnier in a completely moronic kind of way. He was serious.

"I'm serious, Loveletter," he said.

I didn't say anything. I tried to figure out if there was a response to the situation, and out of some kind of misplaced optimism, I tried to act one out. I sat in my desk chair and pretended to be a guy who wanted to do homework. I examined my stepfather's annual report picture and tried to figure out where I could put it so that it would be safe. Suddenly Steve's shadow crossed the page, and I felt a current of disproportionate fear sweep over me. I'd been manhandled hundreds of times before, had my underwear pulled up and hooked on the hand dryer in the bathroom, my food tray hip-checked out of my hands into the stratosphere of the dining hall. I'd been tripped on my way into the shower, knocked down flights of stairs in the rush to get out of class, and thrown into the ornamental shrubs on a nearly daily basis. And for all these reasons, I turned and punched Steve in the stomach with as much strength as I could gather into my pretty small fist. I hit him hard enough to knock a little poof of air out of his mouth. I was kind of impressed by how much violence I had managed to muster, though a little embarrassed that I had mustered it.

"Why did you do that?" he asked, sounding more stunned than hurt, more curious than actually physically wounded.

Don't murder me, I thought. Please don't murder me. I closed my eyes and put my hands over my head, but nothing happened. By some miracle, Steve and the team decided to let the incident pass as the action of a clowning freak. The hockey players laughed so hard that guys in a four-room radius had to know how fucked up everyone was, sitting in our room with Todd's hookah still going around. I pulled my hands back down and put them in my pockets where they were safe. Everybody was going at it, ha-ha-ing their heads off. Todd and Kenny J. looked as if they had gotten into the acid in the mini-fridge, that's how twisted and deranged their faces were: Their mouths stuck open, tears coming out their eyes, cheeks bright red. It was a hell of a distortion.

"You know, you are one fucked-up little freak," hockey player number 8 observed.

Kenny J. put a hand over his right eye.

"Camera One," he said.

He switched hands, putting the other hand over his left eye.

"Camera Two," he said.

There was no explaining Kenny J. He kept up the business with his hands, Camera One, Camera Two, until he had all the rest of them doing it, changing their perspectives on solid objects in the room with the left-right of their vision.

"Cool," Kenny J. said, Camera One, Camera Two–ing me.

Kenny J. had said "cool" fourteen times that day already. The dude could have stocked a few more adjectives in his arsenal. Todd was sitting all by himself across from my bed, smiling harder than I'd ever seen him smile—so hard I knew he had to have been making some money. The room felt crowded, and then Steve got up and ground his knuckles into my head, performing a maneuver called a noogie. Just as if he were one tentacle of an octopus, every other hockey player performed the same ritual. I am going to be bald someday as a result of fraternizing with hockey players.

"Quit it," I said.

I was feeling uptight. In every room people gather in to smoke dope, there is always one guy who doesn't feel the love or get the joke, and that day I was the guy. I was the dude without the sense of humor, a fate I usually did my damnedest to avoid by ingesting more chemicals than I could physically tolerate. There is nothing funnier than a guy who wakes up in the middle of the night screaming because he's just dreamed he's grown a tail, or than a guy who falls asleep in class and wakes up with drool smeared all over his face. I always tried to be that guy, and yet, somehow, I had turned into the other guy, the one who didn't get the humor of the humiliating situation. The only way to get past it was to smoke more dope.

Todd stood up and tacked my picture of Knees up on the wall next to his postcard. As I looked up at it, I got to thinking about how Knees's kind of old-fashioned sincerity wasn't all that prevalent in the world, and it broke my heart to be losing my proximity to it. I felt his eyes on me, pinked earlier by my highlighter pen and twice as world-weary. I wondered what advice he might hand down at this moment and decided that it would have to do with perseverance, which he felt was one of the most important reasons for his success in the banking business.

Perseverance, I decided without looking in a diction-
ary, was a word that implied getting more baked. I got up
from the floor and squeezed in between the hockey team
and onto my bed. Todd packed the bowl of the hookah
and passed it to me, along with the translucent yellow
lighter we had found on the sidewalk one day when we
had skipped out to Dunkin' Donuts. The dope whirled
its way up the hookah, but before I could get the full hit
into my system, the bed groaned and the metal frame
seemed to drop out from underneath us. Then a crack
like a pebble makes when it hits a windshield split the air.
One minute I was deciding to inhale, the smell of dope in
my nostrils and throat, my brain cells doing a little dance,
and the next minute I was sitting on the floor in a pile of
hockey players and broken glass. The pace of destiny isn't
designed to give a guy a break. As near as I could tell, I
was on this planet to suffer and suffer mightily.

The bed collapsed under the weight of me, Kenny J.,
and four big hockey players, turning Haley the goldfish
into a fishwich. At first, everyone laughed—Kenny J., me,
Todd, and the four hockey players. We laughed so hard our
insides almost fell out. Me and the hockey players—five
of us guys, holding our stomachs and snorting out our

noses. It was the first time I had gotten to laughing hard in a while and it was like a wind was blowing up through me and pushing my entire being out. I felt like I was finally in on something and it was funnier than hell. We all laughed so hard that we forgot what we were laughing at. The bong tipped over, and bong water mixed with fish water and beer on the gray industrial carpet. Less than a minute later, Robert Jones, the pencil-necked hall monitor, was at the door in a terry robe that was too big for him and a pair of rubber flip-flops that looked like they had once belonged to a girl and had since had the flower pulled off the top. Under his arm, he carried a basket full of shower supplies, including, and I'm not kidding, a plastic razor and a can of shaving cream.

"What are you smiling at?" Robert asked, crooking his finger in my direction.

He looked at each of us, and nobody said anything. We were distracted by his winkie, which was looking like it wanted to peek out of his robe. If his winkie was anything like his neck, it was bound to be insubstantial, though I'd seen guys with less build on them than Robert who had some kind of uncommon growth in the area in question. I'm not saying I'm one of those guys. I'm just saying that I'd seen it happen, that's all—and, no, I didn't go around looking. Nobody at Stillwater went around looking if they knew what was good for them. If, in the unfortunate case, a guy got trapped alone with another naked guy, it was considered good manners to spend the time counting wall tiles.

The tape deck switched directions and Jerry sang, "Bertha, don't you come around here anymore."

"Is that an unauthorized pet?" Robert noticed the wet, twitching mess on the floor. Haley, after the force of the impact, had spurted out from under the bed.

"A dead one," Todd said.

Todd slid Haley onto one of his computer disks. One eye had turned bone colored, and the other one looked as if it had been put in a blender. Haley's tail had lost its luminosity, so now instead of looking like the comet he had been named after, he looked more like something you would clean from the inside of your microwave oven after thawing a frozen pizza. The thing is, we really liked Haley. Once in a while, I scrubbed the scum off the inside of his bowl with a toilet brush and put him in the window for a little daylight. Other times, I just sat him on my desk and looked at him circling his plastic plant.

Todd enclosed what was left of him in Robert's yellow soap container, which we had borrowed from his basket more or less against his will. Meanwhile, the tragedy killed the party. Their hands in their pockets, their legs a little wobbly from the afternoon's ingestion of chemicals, the hockey players got up and staggered away. Outside our window, the sun made a last grasp with its orange fingers around the tapestry before dipping into the horizon.

"Burial at sea," Kenny J. suggested.

Todd put a different tape in the deck, not one of my bootlegs but an actual album with a studio recording of "Althea." Then he signaled for me to follow and started down the hall. The music trailed behind our procession— Kenny J., me, and Todd followed by Robert, who was still on his way to take his shower. I held the bathroom door open for Todd, and Todd opened the yellow plastic dish that was Haley's coffin one last time. Steam had collected on the mirrors and on the metal faces of the towel dispensers and had shrouded the place in a spooky fog. We splashed through small puddles on the tile floor and I wished I had remembered to wear my flip-flops, too. We were all being eaten from the bottom up by an athlete's foot fungus that had a legacy at Stillwater older than the oldest alumni, a legacy probably stretching back to the founder himself. I bet you there are guys out there with grandfathers with the same strain of athlete's foot as me. I bet some of the worst sufferers sit around their country clubs drinking Scotch whisky, reminiscing about the stuff that grew on their feet, talking about it as if it were the best damn thing that had ever happened to them, as if those were the days.

"I want my soap thing back when you're done," Robert whined.

Todd pointed his trigger finger, firing an imaginary bullet that lodged in an imaginary space deep inside the guy's brain.

"Bang," he said.

Robert let go of his elbows, surprised. The poor guy suddenly got that his days as authority figure were numbered. We all knew what was going to happen next. It'd happened plenty of times before. First, he'd write us up for the unauthorized pet. The hall monitor was nothing if not diligent. Most guys would have picked up on the dope seeds lying around our room, the smell, and the I'm-fucked-now look on the hockey players' faces, but not Robert Jones: He was out to bust bigger crimes, smite sloppiness wherever it presented itself, sniff out the violations of dirty laundry, old food containers, and dead fish. They trained these guys at Stillwater, handpicked them as freshmen to be the partially blind, lousy, rat-fink snitches they almost always were.

If he cared to look, there was enough contraband in our room to get us sent to reform school and out of his hair for life: two sheets of windowpane acid in the mini-fridge and the still slightly smoking hookah in the closet. Once the hall monitor had finished finking on us for the safe stuff, the proctor would take over. "One day, you will take this prankishness of yours too far," he would say, as a way of warming up. The proctor was a tired old guy in his midfifties, with laugh lines around his eyes, a deep, saggy face, and thick black hair that didn't seem to fall out or gray despite the obvious stress he was under.

I had gotten out of the habit of listening to the proctor, but even so, he would rattle on as if the school paid him his big bucks to make dire predictions about our future. He'd hold on to the desk in front of him with both hands, leaning forward across it to look us in the eye. I think he liked making Todd and me feel like we were dragging him out of his apartment in his bathrobe and a pair of old slippers with holes in the toe. He'd hang on to his dignity as we gave him our entire explanation, a series of excuses that didn't amount to much. He'd untie and tie the front of his robe a few times, slap back and forth across the oak floor. Boarding-school proctors must be the only guys in the world who still wear pajamas with white piping—they must have a special store somewhere just for them.

"You are not so much a redeemable troublemaker," he'd say to me, "as a potential flaw in the machine." With Todd, he always led off with the label of "poor influence." Once he had our official designations established, he'd send us back to our room to reflect on our actions. We'd smoke more dope and joke about either slipping a hit of acid into the hall monitor's milk at dinner or transferring a dead frog from the biology laboratory to his pillow, whatever we figured would mess with his head worse.

Life is hair-trigger, man; it can go off at any time and blow you all to pieces. It's a mistake to forget that.

I depressed the handle on the toilet. The sound of the water, Haley swirling down, subtle and final. The music from our tape deck pumped softly down the hall behind us—Jerry singing and the acoustic strumming, pulsing in the air like the beat of a giant, mellow heart. Soft words, water rushing, the passing of one fluid moment in time.

Jerry had the voice to express what I felt when I said good-bye. The moment, like a bead of water, seemed suspended above the pool of my many happy memories of Haley. I'd probably get another goldfish. I'd probably not think too much about him ever again. I had no way of knowing, though, since all of my feelings about Haley, Knees, the dope I had smoked, and my friendship with Steve had eddied together and the only one I could hold on to was somewhere down the hall coming from the tape deck, changing, wafting, becoming something else.

Tragedies are like photographs taken when your eyes are still closed or like the click and freezing of film as it slips on a reel. Ask a fifty-seven-year-old guy like my stepfather Knees where he was when Kennedy was shot and he'll tell you everything from the color of the coffee cup he was holding to the weather that was pattering his window. He'll tell you stuff that has nothing to do with anything, and then he'll get this expression on his face, a crease along his forehead, a fogginess behind his eyeglasses.

"Those were dangerous times," he'll say, reliving the whole thing, and then he'll stop, change the subject. The picture will reshuffle to the back of his mind, and he'll move on to something else, never quite looking at you again.

EYES OF THE
WORLD

THE PROCTOR PROGNOSTICATED and punished us even more tiredly than I had predicted and I got a night's sleep that might have been good, though there seemed to be no concrete evidence like clearer thoughts or brighter eyes to prove it the next morning. Meanwhile, I decided to give up smoking dope forever, or for at least as long as it took to find out whether my mother was coming for Parents' Weekend. Some of the time I spent at Stillwater was like that—me wandering around with too many good intentions for the situation at hand. If the preceding day was a rough one—and after the murder of my goldfish, I could honestly say that it was—then I got out of bed the next morning optimistic, ready to work on my karma. It didn't take me five minutes of thinking happy thoughts before reality took me in its teeth again. I got up to feed Haley, pulled his cracked and empty bowl out from under my propped-up bed, and suddenly had a flashback, a vision of Haley's mangled body curled up in the soap holder we had used as a coffin, his ventral fins rising up before me, his scales drying up at the edges. I couldn't believe what my synapses were telling me. I remembered the proctor's prediction of no place to go for miscreants of Todd's and my caliber. My hands started to shake, and I climbed back under the covers.

Todd was still down for the count, not even under his covers but sleeping half dressed, his face buried in his pillow. During the night, the baseboard vents had blasted out so much heat that beads of sweat rolled down the walls, and something smelled on my side of the room that was even more evil than spilled bong water. Because we had the shades drawn and our tapestry shut, it was impossible to tell what time of day it was. A touch of gray peered in around the edges of the window, but only someone more experienced in the nuances of morning could have deciphered what that meant. I closed my eyes for what seemed like two more minutes, and when I opened them again, Todd was gone. In fact, the whole dorm resonated with an eerie silence, and I realized I must have slept through something important.

Panic set in, and I rushed around to get myself together, grabbing my oxford shirt and fumbling with the buttons. School muumuus or caftans might have been better choices of uniform for guys as deficient as I was in the art of zipping and tucking. I searched around and found an almost-clean pair of pants, my blazer, and my blue peacoat lying on the floor of the closet. Once I was dressed, I busted my way out the door and down the stairs as fast as a guy in my condition could move.

I had to slow down outside so as not to slip and knock myself into the ornamental shrubbery and pick up more stains. The snow had melted and frozen and melted again so that the mounds along the shoveled walks were streaked with black rivers. The trees had buckled underneath ice, but a couple of intrepid limbs had broken free and tossed twigs and pine needles, making the quad look like a ballroom littered by New Year's revelers who since had returned home to nurse their hangovers. The administration liked to have the campus looking nice for

Parents' Weekend—blue skies, clear walkways, dormant ivy vines climbing up the brick faces of the buildings, not just for the parents, but for the bulletins and catalogs, for the calendars they sent out every spring to get their funding. The weather had made scene-setting tricky.

As I made my way over to the dining hall, two things kept nagging at me: the snow sticking to my socks and the feeling that Todd had snuck out of the dorm without waking me for a reason. I owed him $220 on account of my mother forgetting to send my allowance checks after our argument. I'd also spilled bong water on his bed and ruined his comforter only a few days earlier. I thought about the tunes I had wanted to hear at Freedom—"Bertha," "Aiko," "Dark Star." Jerry almost never played "Dark Star." Todd would charge me a fortune for the Freedom tape if Jerry played "Dark Star" and probably wouldn't let me buy it on credit.

After veering off the main walkway, I trudged across a path of thawed mud that had been churned by people who had shortcutted across the grass earlier. All the dead turf and trampled snow around the campus was a testament to the cutthroat world Stillwater was preparing its students for once they graduated. As a protest, I tried my first winter to stick to the shoveled routes, but I ended up late and had to settle for meat loaf and Brussels sprouts in the dining hall and to stay ten minutes after every class. I eventually started leaving the walkways every chance I got, too—to hell with school pride and kindness to green space.

The cars parked one behind the other on the circular drive suggested that it might be about twelve-thirty—past time for the beginning of the big Parents' Weekend shindig but not too late for the main meal. Despite the snow and salty roads, each car looked better than the last—shinier, more entitled to the spot it had taken, more like it had spent a comfortable night in a heated garage. I counted four Mercedes, two Jaguars, seven minivans, and a six-pack of Volvos. If Linda had arrived, her car would have been left double parked in front of the dining hall, the engine still running, Joseph the chauffeur picking his nose in the front seat. Linda liked to make an entrance, and tripping her way through snowbanks to eat cafeteria food just wasn't her style.

By the time I got to the dining hall, my shoes had filled so full of snow I sloshed when I walked and the cuffs of my khakis were stained a dark brown exhaust color. If I had a polite bone in my body, I might have worn boots and changed into shoes when I got inside, but then I would have been even later, and chances are somebody would have noticed and written me up.

I searched the vestibule and slalomed through a group of other people's parents clucking over their half-full coffee cups about the problems they thought their sons had had adjusting. I overheard the mother of one of the yearbook staffers (she looked just like the idiot) telling another mother about how her kid had had his wet clothes stolen out of the washing machine and tossed out the window. Her kid had taken overly candid photographs of a performance of *A Midsummer Night's Dream*, and she entertained her circle with inaccurate and unfair observations about the incident. I don't care who you are—it's not easy to wear tights in public, and the acting club wasn't "an aggressive bunch of ruffians." She seemed to miss what an obvious pain in the ass her son had been, sneaking up on those poor tights-wearing thespians. I gave the woman in question a dirty look, but I was too late. The other parents had formed a support group.

"That's awful," one of the circle said consolingly.

"You ought to speak to somebody."

It got so bad, I left them and sat down on a bench in the corner. I pulled off my shoes, dumped the snow out of them, and shook the smell out of my wet socks, stuffing them into my blazer pockets.

"Hi," I said to somebody's father on the other side of the bench. He had been watching me, but when I spoke to him he glanced away.

"Do you know what time it is?" I asked, just to keep the talk going.

"No," he said.

"You're Spec's dad, aren't you?" I asked him—his back, actually, since he had almost completely turned around.

"Excuse me?"

"You're one of Cameron Spector's fathers?" The guy had once taken us all out for lunch, but apparently he had forgotten or had other things on his mind.

"His only one, actually," the guy said.

"No kidding." I forgot my bare feet for a minute.

Now that he mentioned it, he did look an awful lot like Spec—the same eyes, the receding hair. He jingled a bunch of change in his pocket and raised his eyebrows as if he were letting me in on some kind of joke and making an escape at the same time. While I put on my shoes without the socks—a painful process—he slipped off the bench and into the main hall. After a minute, I limped in the same direction.

It was already past Thanksgiving and not yet Christmas and the last thing any sane person wanted to be reminded of was turkey, but even so the theme of this year's Parents' Weekend was Turkey Madness. In the main hall, the entertainment committee had worked overtime building the centerpieces, hanging orange and brown streamers and a WELCOME, PARENTS sign. The administration had done some gilding of their own, adding a giant ice sculpture and a champagne fountain, a string trio, and a fleet of rented servers wearing orange cummerbunds and bow ties. They had hidden the regular toothless and hairnetted kitchen ladies in the back for the festivities. The faculty members had decked themselves out in their absolute finery. Even the young, "hip" instructors had pulled their hair back and wore ties—some of them Jerry Garcia prints, as a matter of fact.

The only free seats I could immediately see were at a round table twenty feet from the entrance where three guys were sitting alone. I guess most people would have called them nerds, although I hate using terms that get their popularity from sitcoms, no matter how accurate they might be. Even the lower circles at Stillwater had their pride, not that it always needed to be respected. The three picked at their meals with their forks. A dangling papier-mâché turkey cast a shadow over them and drew attention to their uneaten mashed potatoes, flattened or shaped into castles on their plates.

The other tables in the hall were occupied by the usual groups (with their families). Along the back wall, the hockey players had staked out six or seven tables. They had recently beat Hotchkiss, and that perhaps explained why they had spent a celebratory night squashing my goldfish. A lot of backslapping and tie grabbing went on where they were sitting, and a lot of bruises of happiness were being delivered by proud parents, older brothers, and cousins. One server with a boat of turkey gravy on his tray backed off to avoid the joyful contact between a grandfather and a grandson. The grandfather looked to be in his eighties, but he delivered his whacks on the back as if he had scored hat tricks his whole life.

In the center of the room, I saw another group: Walter Hackett and his family dressed in Sunday clothes and shined shoes. Even the littlest Hackett had a tie on, poor kid. Walter was a townie, which meant that he almost never took meals on campus and didn't know any better than to seem like he was attending church. His family made a warm spot in their violets and grays and whites, a place where the power had been turned down and a guy could find respite from the corporate-power-wielding blue suits and browbeating ties.

I had once had dinner at Walt's house. Todd was Walt's biology lab partner, and I guess Walt thought goodwill had grown between them, at least before he caught on that we were mostly using him and his beat-up Camaro for rides off campus. It was a weird experience, all of us sitting together in the Hacketts' kitchen, eating food that they had prepared themselves. The house felt crowded without a library or an arboretum, a dining room to eat in or a breakfast nook. I knew some people could talk to each other from anyplace inside their house without the use of intercoms; I had just never had the chance to experience it personally before. My favorite room was the kitchen. While I sat talking to Walt's mom, the littlest Hackett fell asleep in my lap and drooled all over my best khakis—the pair with the smallest number of shrubbery stains. I couldn't bear to push the kid off. His head was warm like my mother's dog Rufus's, heavy in my lap without being too heavy.

As sweet as that little Hackett was, I decided not to join Walt because I would have had to pass right in front of the proctor and the headmaster with my socks stuffed into my blazer. The headmaster might have missed that I was forty-five minutes late for the meal, but he wouldn't have forgotten my mother or what a visit from her on a money-earning day might mean to the prosperity of the school. He wore a look of intense joy on his face, the kind of illumination he got every year around donation time. I knew he was in the mood to single me out for some special attention. Knees, he had figured out, had been a regular check signer from the very first, and the headmaster had a love affair going with him, my mother, and my trust fund. What he didn't know was that the plug had been pulled and Knees was history, just like everyone else in the line of wealthy stepdads before him. My mother was liable to be just as ungenerous as Knees had been generous, not because she had less money, but because she was forgetful about things like paying bills, offering up gratitude, and sending my allowance check on time.

Noticeably absent from the hall were the families of any of the freak brigade, but the draw of the Freedom show more than likely was the explanation, that and the usual accessories—earrings and bandannas—were scuttled for the day. Also, freaks don't have as stable families as some of the other subgroups, so perhaps, like Todd, they had used their orphanhood as an excuse to ditch. The lack of compadres meant that I had no choice but to settle in with the weird, lonely guys under the turkey who appeared not to have any parents or family members willing to own up to their relationship with them either. My feet were killing me. Sitting with them was better than having another blister pop.

Just as I landed, a loud roar erupted from the hockey player section. I looked up and spotted Steve messing with the head of a smaller version of himself. A woman who must have been his mother sat in the chair next to him, blond angled hair falling over her face. She looked like Steve, too—everyone in the family looked like their name could be Steve, including his girlfriend sitting on the other side of mini-Steve. While I took my place with the lowest of the low, the social zeros, I wondered what it would be like not to feel like a wallflower hanging out by the water fountain at a dance. The guys at my table were having a discussion that required them to use math words like *compute* and *triangulate*, words designed to alienate, in my opinion. What is it about lonely guys that makes you feel lonelier? The guy sitting in the seat next to me had a face that was downright sensitive. He drew on the middle of his napkin with a ballpoint pen, constructing a platform with an upside-down **L** shape and a rope coming down. He tore at the paper and speckled his hand with ink.

"Want to play hangman?" he asked me.

"Are you kidding?" I scooted my chair farther over and raised my eyebrows. I must have mastered the expression with innate genius. The guy with the pen set it aside and looked even more hurt.

"Hey, just asking," he said.

Another guy, a Japanese guy, peered at the five blank lines underneath the drawing on the wrinkled napkin. His face compressed and expanded again as if a lightbulb had been flicked on in his head. "*Z*," he suggested—not a more likely letter, like *E* or *S* or *T*, that a person more experienced with the game of hangman or the English language might have guessed. He leaned over the table and held a corner of the napkin down so that he could see. Sad little Leaky Pen wiped his hand across his nose. Finally he bore down and filled in the letter *Z* in the first of the five slots. I served myself some of what was left of the cold mashed potatoes and flattened them out on my plate.

"Zebra," the Japanese guy blurted out.

Who'd have thought that a Japanese guy would have gotten a word like *zebra* on the first try—although for all I know they've got herds and herds of zebras in Japan. A girl laughed from the direction of the hockey team's tables. They let plenty of girls in on Parents' Weekend—girlfriends, sisters, the occasional stepmother—and they had a way of changing the atmosphere. Normally everyone ate with their heads down, food taking the shortest possible path to digestion, but on Parents' Weekend people rose from their seats to get extra cups of coffee from the urn and to pass plates to the waiters. The activity bypassed our table as if we were the one motor home in a motor park not destined to take a spiral path to Oz. A real beauty of a girl with a French braid sailed through without even looking our way. It always took a while for me to get used to the presence of girls, as limited as I was in my experience with them. I was afraid they were going to do something mean—make fun of me, or treat me like dirt—like the hockey players did, only worse.

Having a girlfriend, participating in some of the things Steve had mentioned during our smoke session—making out in the back of a car or down at the horse barn—but also doing some other things, things like laying my head in a girl's lap or brushing her hair, were dreams I dared not dream. I would need some kind of manual to get started, and I'd be damned if I would use one of my mother's books. I had been around her editing process and I had learned the eighteen surefire ways to make a woman sing, and the nineteenth technique, which had been left on the cutting-room floor, but I was stunned when it came to girls, more interested in love than sex, which at Stillwater made me a perverse young dude, really.

"New game," Leaky Pen said, interrupting my thoughts.

He flipped the napkin over and constructed another set of lines and another scaffold. From what I could tell, the Japanese guy was the only one of the group with a reason to be alone on Parents' Weekend, who wasn't quite as big a loser as the rest of us, although I wondered why he wasn't upstairs playing poker with the other foreign guys whose parents weren't coming. Even though they didn't all speak the same language, the foreign guys at Stillwater had a club. They could get to laughing and talking, and nobody else knew what the heck was going on with them—the inside-joke syndrome. Foreign guys seemed to run around happy over nothing, going crazy over nonsense. Maybe being three thousand miles from home and family could make a guy a little giddy.

"Hey, Loveletter . . ."

On the other side of the table, a fat guy I knew from geometry class scooped some buttered peas from a serving dish and handed them in my direction. I considered reminding him that I had a real last name—Emerson-Fitzgerald or Douglas—but as I wasn't sure which one applied, I let my mother's stupid alias pass. Everyone at the table was polite and doing their damnedest not to embarrass me. It's amazing how much arrogance a bunch of zeros can work up once they start running together. If my mother had entered the room just then, she wouldn't have looked for me at my table full of geeks—the guy with the leaky pen with his hand resting on his paper napkin, the Japanese guy screwing up his face trying to guess another word. If she had shown up, she would have looked right over our heads to the tables with the heavy hitters and the backslappers. There would have been a pause while I tried to get her attention, and then her chin would have come down and her eyes would have focused. I could practically hear her disappointed sigh.

She was always neediest of the bright lights during her temporarily single phases, always more restless about finding the limelight. The April before last, we hopped a jet to Las Vegas to file her dissolution papers from Fitzgerald, and then we stayed a few days and saw the show with the sedated white tigers. It was a hell of a visit, one of those times my mother treated me more as a lover than a son and let me see her as flirtatious, silly. She chased off a guy who hit on her in the airport lounge and focused on me, pledging to remain single for more than five minutes and grabbing my hand across the table in order to apologize with her eyes. If she had arrived for Parents' Weekend, she might have settled for backslapping but sadly not hangman under a turkey, since everything about the dudes at my table screamed sorry in a direct way.

I wasn't the only guy at Stillwater who had issues with his mother. All of us at Stillwater were virtual orphans, sadder in condition than any Disney character or that snot nose who yammers about figgy pudding in one of Scrooge's Christmas scenarios, that "God Bless Us Every One" loser. I had blown my moment to take another Vegas trip to divorce Knees the moment I hinted that at her age she might get a better media reaction from a photo shoot for *Family Circle* than for *Playboy*. I didn't mean it, exactly. I just thought I personally would like to see her in an apron, rather than nothing at all, and that I might not be the only guy. As a result, it was looking like it might not be until Christmas before I saw her again—hell, it not might be until after the New Year, when I and everyone I knew would have to pull a staple out of her belly button to see her completely.

I lifted Leaky Pen's wrist and checked his watch, just in case I had the time mixed up. His hand dropped to the table, upsetting a pile of comment cards left by the catering crew, little canary-colored rectangles with HOW CAN WE SERVE YOU BETTER? printed on the front. The sad thing was I actually did have a comment for whoever made the buttered peas, and it was that they sucked. I didn't write it down, though, because I was still watching the door, and more than likely it was the kitchen staff who would be held responsible, and they had a thing against me already. I waited five more minutes. The guys at the geek table were just as invisible as I felt when my mother wasn't seeing me. I had been in a half dozen classes with the one guy with the peas and still I couldn't remember his name. He pointed his spoon at me like it was the pipe he might have been photographed with on the back of a book jacket.

"Your family not coming either, Loveletter?" he asked me.

I hated it when anyone called me "Loveletter." I would have even preferred "homo" if it was said kindly enough, because at least "homo" still meant human being, but the guy was trying, I had to give him that. Most guys in his position would have seen the futility of their efforts long ago.

"You bet my family's coming," I answered Peas Passer.

I saw something flicker between him and the Japanese guy, an understanding that they weren't going to contradict me even if I started raving like a lunatic. Had I been more pugilistic, I might have gotten up and stuck their faces in the mashed potatoes. The guy with the leaky pen kept working on his napkin and ignored the smoke practically pouring out of my ears. He was drawing the spaces and another scaffold for a word with eleven letters. Todd had the right idea, skipping all this. He was probably halfway to Freedom already, plastered on the same drugs he would give the hall monitor as revenge for the trouble he had caused us the night before. I looked down at Leaky Pen's letter blanks and made a guess.

"*E*," I said, just to go with something obvious and get everyone off my back.

"*E*?" Leaky Pen asked.

It seemed like a logical choice. Leaky Pen was surprised that I had jumped in, but in order not to miss the chance to include me, he drew a head on his napkin and wrote the letter *E* down in the miss column. I think he was relieved to find himself playing with somebody other than the Japanese guy, who seemed to have some kind of uncanny hangman genius. He cleared a space around the napkin so we all could see and handed a pitcher of iced tea to Peas Passer, who put it at his side of the table. I felt bad for the Japanese guy. He obviously wanted to play, but nobody likes to play games with people as smart as him.

"Will you introduce me to Linda?" Peas Passer asked. He picked up a spoon and began tapping it nervously on the oak table.

Everyone else looked up.

"Sure," I said, although there was nothing sure about it.

"Really?" Peas Passer asked, not quite believing me.

"Sure," I said again. "She would really enjoy making your acquaintance."

Old Peas Passer looked like he might wet himself right there. And though it was causing him a coronary, it wasn't such a far-fetched idea. Give him about forty years and a couple million dollars and Peas Passer might actually be my mother's type. He was as boring as either of my first two steps, and since my mother always subscribed to the theory that opposites are the most attractive, his repulsiveness stood him in good stead. I thought about having Peas Passer as family and pushed the mashed potatoes to a safe distance, nearer to the Japanese guy. Peas Passer's face turned a couple of different colors at the thought of meeting my mother, and then he finally figured out I was messing with him.

But I couldn't get the idea of him as a dad out of

my thoughts. Maybe it was the spoon that had made me think of a pipe and his *Father Knows Best* superiority. We would make an interesting family of four, sitting around our table having a family game hour. The Japanese guy would be our oldest, the pride and joy, a chip off the old block. Leaky Pen would sadly have to take the role of impish little sister, and I was a shoo-in for Mom because of how I indulged these guys, how I put up with them even though I had better places to be.

"Try the letter *F*," the Japanese guy advised.

"*F*," I said.

The guy with the leaky pen wrote down the letter *F* on the first blank.

Somewhere in the room, someone clinked a fork against a glass, a signal that the bullshit part of lunch was about to begin, the time to take out hearing aids if you had them. The headmaster slid his chair back from the faculty table and made a short speech about patriotism and school spirit. He emphasized that we were all good Americans and that Stillwater would help us grow up to be fine adults. He mentioned a couple of alumni who had really made it after Stillwater: the guy who had served as undersecretary in charge of campaign contributions for some damn fascist administration and another guy who made a half billion inventing spray-on cheese. Afterward, he began to circulate among the tables just to the right of ours, shaking the hands of as many father-mother-banker-lawyer types as he thought could write a check.

Lunch was just about over. If my mother were going to show up, she was going to be too late to eat and hopefully too late to shake the headmaster's hand, although that might have been overly optimistic. The headmaster kept on shaking until he found himself in a corner along the portrait wall and next to the hockey team and their families, whereupon he switched to backslapping. The backslapping seemed to come easier to him, more his natural style. He was probably turning up the checks he was looking for—donations to the science lab and for tennis team uniforms, money to send a group of hockey players to sports camp next summer.

I had to admit, except for the buttered peas, the administration really did turn out an impressive spread when they put their mind to it. Now that dinner was over, the hired catering crew distributed brandy and champagne in long-stemmed glasses to each adult. The string trio plucked out a little sonic wallpaper, and the headmaster had the dinner plates cleared away. Three guys in matching cummerbunds rolled out a giant cake constructed to look like the Marilyn Quayle Gymnasium, each floor supported by toothpicks and each window illuminated by yellow frosting. A few people applauded and actually got out of their seats to look at the masterpiece before the waiter in charge sliced it to pieces. All the while, the headmaster kept smiling and circulating. If he'd had a tail, I'm sure he would have wagged it.

"*N*." I guessed a letter of Leaky Pen's puzzle.

If anyone at my table had been distracted by the clinking of glasses, the light patter and subsequent hearty laughter of other people's deal-making parents, they didn't show it. A waiter with a napkin over his tray arrived with slices of cake, but Peas Passer was the only one of us to take one. Leaky Pen carefully drew the letter *N* in the fourth blank of the puzzle, and we moved around on our chairs, getting closer to the napkin and warming up for the next assault. Among the three of us—Peas Passer, the Japanese guy, and me—we had guessed all but three of the letters so that the puzzle read FORN _ _ AT _ ON. We had also worked our way up to a hanging guy with a full set of clothes, boots, and anatomically correct hands.

Out of generosity, Leaky Pen allowed facial hair and eye-glasses. We had only a couple more guesses before the game was up. I felt the pressure building.

I squinted at the puzzle and guessed the letter *I* and then suddenly everything became clear. "Fornication!" I shouted. The members of the string trio had taken that moment to lay down their instruments, and so my voice rang out and echoed in the full hall. They probably even heard me at the Hackett table; I hoped Walt's mother had time to put her hands over the ears of the littlest Hackett. I loved that little guy.

"I beg your pardon, Mr., um—?" the headmaster hesitated, searching for the correct surname.

Leaky Pen sat up and flipped the napkin over. Both the Japanese guy and Peas Passer slid down the bench in the other direction. The headmaster, used to dealing with me and under the scrutiny of his public, decided to handle the matter calmly, meaning he pulled out a small notebook and wrote one of my names in it, a sure sign a subordinate would be out to harass me later.

"And where is your family, Mr.—" He coughed. "Weren't we expecting your mother or father?" He stood right behind me, his hand extended as if permanently stuck in the shaking position.

"She's late, sir," I said.

I should have known he was going to be at our table eventually, doing his number on us. The guys I was sitting with might not have looked like much, but even I had to admit, after getting to know them, that they represented a certain kind of future fiscal potential. The Japanese guy, especially, had a pretty remarkable puzzle-solving ability. Within ten years, he'd be in and out of MIT, making close to five times what the headmaster was making now. He had NEW SCIENCE LAB written all over him.

With his right hand, the headmaster grabbed me by my right hand and then held my elbow in a grip with his left while he made eye contact. He had to have had the wettest hands of anybody I had ever met, pure seaweed, probably a result of overuse. I winced when he touched me, although because I had nothing against the guy, I tried not to let him see me. Assertive handshaking is the kind of thing they teach you at Stillwater and expect you to practice the rest of your life. According to textbooks on the subject, handshakes can make or break you. I couldn't manage the stare, grip, and press in the right order. My hands started to feel like trained doves fluttering toward the rafters before the magician finishes the trick.

"I know how much you will miss her," the headmaster said.

He leaned hard on the sympathy, getting it into his voice and almost making it sound sincere. Then he moved away from me and completed his ritual around the table, taking a hand and telling each owner, "I know how much you miss them." When he had come all the way to the other side, he took the Japanese guy's hand and said the same thing in Japanese. I was the first person to rag on the headmaster for being more sensitive to the school's financial state than the students' emotional ones, but in the headmaster's world, new lacrosse sticks and a bigger gymnasium meant happiness. In his own way, I could tell, he really was trying to make us feel better. Everyone at Stillwater got homesick once in a while. Who wouldn't when home is a forty-room house or a château in France? The headmaster was probably homesick for my house, too.

A definite silence fell over the table after the head-master had come, shaken, and gone. Leaky Pen turned his napkin back over but didn't write anything. Peas Passer picked up his spoon and began tapping again.

"What would you know about fornication, Love-letter?" he asked. Like a good dad, he was trying to shift the mood.

"That was funny . . . " the Japanese guy began.

I looked at him. He started to talk faster.

"That was funny, Mr. Reynolds coming up behind."

All three of them laughed, but not well—out their noses, "snee, snee, snee," with their hands up over their mouths, too much body movement, and no eyebrow control. They looked at me, not so much as if I were what they were laughing at, but more like I was responsible for them laughing at all. I made a face and they all stopped, and then I smiled and they started again. I finally had to yank the spoon right out of Peas Passer's hand to make him stop tapping it. It's a warm feeling, being laughed at by nerds. They are a lot gentler about it, a lot more shy and deferential than Todd and Steve and the hockey team. A warmth came over me the way it sometimes did when I was listening to Jerry, as if this extra and unexpected serving of family life could bolster me and get me through the difficult times ahead.

We made a touching nuclear family, it was true, but

I also felt squared off, tossed into another box. Jerry preached the gospel of the human family and I believed in the directive despite the trouble I had acting on it. The best times were when I listened to Jerry's music. Then buds opened, petals unfolded, broke open, and caught on the wind. The guys at my table looked so happy to be together. Their brains were sharp. Their thoughts clear. I was pulled their way, and maybe it was the dope I hadn't smoked but I felt sharp, too.

At two-fifteen, the handshaking and fundraising finally ground to a halt. Most of the parents left with their sons to inspect the dormitory and refold clothes before the exhibition game down in the hockey arena. The four of us kept our seats until the catering crew members cleared everything they could get their hands on off the table, including the comment cards and the stack of used napkins we had used to play our game.

"*R*," the Japanese guy guessed within seconds of me setting up a scaffold on our last napkin. I filled in two *R*s in the middle of my five-letter word.

Leaky Pen leaned in, but before he could speak the Japanese guy guessed my word.

"Jerry!" he shouted.

"That's not a legal word, Loveletter," Peas Passer complained. "That's a proper noun."

"It counts," protested Leaky Pen, who was now Inky Fingers.

"You guys cheat." Peas Passer sulked.

"Do not."

"I win," the Japanese guy said, and threw his hands up in the air.

Even though the string quartet had been replaced by disco hits from the seventies in a boom box, a signal that the catering crew was willing to endure anything to have us leave, we stuck around to play one more game, letting the Japanese guy take a chance with the pen this time. Right away, he came up with a word eight letters long. We figured out that the first letter was *H*, but after a while, I swear we guessed everything from *A* to *Z*. He kept shaking his head and smiling a mad smile that kept getting wider until he had hanged us all three times over at least. Peas Passer was the most pissed off. He leaned his cheek on his hand and sighed; his eyes rolled toward the ceiling in disgust.

"This is the last time I play hangman in a foreign language," he said.

"The word is *hankachu*," the Japanese guy said, proud of himself.

"*Hankachu?*" we asked.

Hankachu turned out to be the Japanese word for handkerchief—not that great a word, but it managed to stump everyone at the table. We all gave the Japanese guy a round of applause and—experimentally, as if we were hockey players—a slap on the back. Even Peas Passer joined in.

"*Hankachu*," Peas Passer complained, shaking his head.

"God bless you," Inky Fingers said, and that terrible laughter started fucking up everyone's faces, mine probably worst of all.

SHAKEDOWN STREET

TWENTY MINUTES LATER, the hangman team and I were out on the lawn, tromping back over to the dorms. Inky Fingers invited me to join them for a game of Risk in his room. Normally world domination wasn't my scene, but I thought, "What the heck." A light fog had settled over the campus while I was inside playing hangman, and the grounds had faded into a pale gray postcard not unlike the November photograph for the last alumni calendar—attractive after all, when the mist hid most of it. The hangman geeks and I lapsed into a discussion of *Star Trek*—one thing geeks and freaks have in common. We were like Jerry's four dancing bears, the

ones on the bumper stickers and T-shirts, smili
feeling that inner happy that only comes once in a while
for no real reason.

The Japanese guy made the point that the *Enterprise*
had no place to take showers, which got me worked up,
too. I argued that it must have had something to do with
evolution, and everyone agreed except Peas Passer. We
joked about how lousy that ship might have stunk a million light-years from anywhere and how it was no wonder
none of them got laid by any green space babes. Something that sounded like a dog moaned from the elm trees
up the road from the dormitories. The snow crackled
underfoot. I still hadn't put my wet socks back on, and
my ankles were chafing.

"Help." An eerie voice broke through the fog.

Peas Passer latched on to the back of my jacket, and
the rest of the hangman team stopped in their tracks.
There were footsteps, almost human, and I shrugged Peas
Passer off and tried to locate where the sound had come
from. A few bullshit stories got passed around every year
about a guy named Three-Fingered Willie who abducted
freshmen, and that's who Peas Passer imagined was waiting to get him. I might have believed in Willie for more

than a minute if there hadn't been stories at my sailing camp of a guy just like him, with two fingers instead of three. There isn't enough scary shit going on in the world but that some people have to go and invent more.

We heard another moan, obviously not a dog this time, and a figure emerged from the gloom, not Three-Fingered Willie, though for a second even I had my doubts. The person seemed to have trouble walking. Peas Passer was hanging on to Inky Fingers now, who was hanging on to the Japanese guy.

"Hello—" Inky Fingers called out, like one of those minor characters in a horror movie.

"Help me," said Robert Jones, the hall monitor from our floor. He staggered into a halo of light cast by a decorative lantern on the side of the dorm. He was wearing only a pair of pajama pants, his flip-flops, and a T-shirt, which looked wet. His forehead was sweaty and his pupils were the size of hockey pucks. He pulled his skinny arms toward his skinny body and stared not at us but at the space that surrounded us.

"Are you OK, dude?" I asked him, though I knew the answer, and knew too that he hadn't woken up with a dead frog from the biology lab under his pillow.

"Loveletter?" he whimpered, recognizing my voice. It took time for his eyes to find me, but once they did, I saw a lot of pain and suffering there. The guy was like Jesus walking out of the desert.

"The bricks," Robert said. He pointed to the ivy-covered wall of the administration building. "They're moving."

Inky Fingers looked over and shook his head, assuring him that all was well. Robert didn't seem convinced, so I tried. "Just think about the Red Stockings," I told him, a baseball team I recalled he liked.

"Sox," he corrected even in his delirium.

I suddenly remembered a lot of other things Robert liked that made me uneasy. I remembered his interest in building rocket models and something about his having gone to Space Camp—tidbits he had shared with us during the first-day assembly when we had to introduce ourselves. Robert Jones was so bright and shiny that day that I could almost see my reflection in his face. It was depressing that all that earnestness had been beaten out in only two months as our hall monitor.

He watched the administration building while the geeks shuffled and pulled their hands out of their pockets. They weren't so socially out of it that they didn't know what had happened. You don't get to be a nerd or a geek at Stillwater by not being skilled at avoiding the worst, and getting on the wrong side of Todd or any of Todd's customers qualified. Peas Passer gave me an accusatory look that I evaded by slapping Robert on the back as if Robert's being dosed were just another hockey player moment. Something unhinged in Robert's shoulders when I touched him. The whirligigs in his brain sped up by a hundred percent. Inky Fingers came up on his other side and Robert's face settled into something I would have called more peaceful if his eyes hadn't look so crazed.

"Oh, I get it," he said. "I get it."

I wondered.

He no longer spoke like the dweeby little hall monitor who had busted Todd and me for the unauthorized pet. He behaved like Kenny J. or me, maybe, after I had eaten the crickets and pepper jack cheese. I wondered when Todd had found the time to sneak Robert the acid, since Todd wasn't at lunch and he hadn't been in the dorm earlier. We usually had a busy schedule the day of a show, with things to pack, stuff to buy. It surprised me that he had actually done what he had said he was going to do, because up until this moment, I had always thought that just letting the guy be the hall monitor was punishment enough. I knew that finding Robert out tripping in the fog was supposed to be funny. I would have to tell the story later as if it was, but I wasn't laughing, not even a single tee-hee. The poor, sad guy was facing a world that would never measure up to the good old days of Space Camp.

"Maybe we should take him back to the dorm," Peas Passer suggested.

Robert explained that he was on his way to the dining hall, though he was three hours too late for lunch and an hour too early for dinner and, no kidding, those dining hall ladies can be mean if you approach them off-hours. I'd been on enough acid trips to know that standing still was tricky, that restraining him would be impossible, and that we were better off letting him find his own way, even if it meant he had to do battle with the demon lunch ladies and the tired catering crew. The bricks on the side of the administration building were drawing him in, and he staggered away from us in their direction. Inky Fingers broke from our group, caught up to him, and gave him his winter jacket. It was a darned sweet thing to do, so kind I wished I'd thought of it, but I pressed on without looking back.

"Have you noticed the thing about the foreheads?" I turned and asked the Japanese guy, hoping to pick up where we had left off, to recapture what had fled from the hangman team's faces the second Robert had made his appearance. A car sputtered up the road from the dormitories. All of my ideas suddenly felt unsteady, the way a fever can make you feel when it sneaks up on you and takes your brain by surprise.

"They take ion showers," Peas Passer said.

"They take what?" I asked.

"Ion showers," he repeated.

He grabbed the front of his jacket and pulled at the sides, looking as serious as my English teacher, like he was going to start quoting *Moby-Dick* and pointing out the metaphorical links between Ishmael and Captain Picard. The car rumbled its way closer, disappearing and reappearing between the trees, a headlight winking at me like a sparkle in Jerry's pupil, becoming Walter Hackett's Camaro, negotiating its way around ten or twenty other cars left in the circular drive in front of the dining hall. I'd seen Walter Hackett leave with his family an hour earlier, yet he was the only guy I knew who'd be brave enough to drive a car that bad—with an orange body, yellow and brown fenders, and a tail pipe that actually dragged on the ground from time to time. I wondered why Walt hadn't gone home, packed out when the rush of Stillwaterites and their parental units had left to watch the hockey game.

"It's a space thing," Peas Passer explained.

"Really?" I said, paying more attention to the car than to Peas Passer, to its single headlight than to his profundity on the topic of *Star Trek*.

"He knows everything about the *Enterprise*," the Japanese guy said, proud for some reason that somebody knew everything about the *Enterprise*.

I put my hands up to shield my eyes from the headlight, which aimed straight at us now. Walt must have recognized me among the members of the varsity hangman team because he slowed down, his tires sloshing puddles along the drive. He bumped to a stop over the curb and onto part of the lawn. I didn't mind Walt finding me with guys outside my usual troupe. He was the least judgmental human I'd ever met. I noticed, though, that in the shadowy back of his car, he had a passenger. My first thought was that his baby brother was back there, but when the car slowed to a stop and the passenger-side door swung open, it was Todd who leaned out from the backseat. He pointed the business end of his grandfather's .45 in my direction.

Todd's gun was so fucking scary it was me who grabbed Peas Passer's coat this time and pushed him in front of me as a human shield. All Todd's other selves I could handle, but not the self that liked to play with guns. Though I'd seen the .45 he was holding before and knew it was a gift from his grandfather, it shook me hard enough that one of my socks fell out of my pocket. It was one thing for him to own a gun and to bring it out one afternoon in our room and show it to me while I was too high to scream or run, but it was another thing to point it at me after the vision of the hall monitor and when my head was as clear and open as the inside of a bell. It was like he was telling me that he was a sociopath and that all this appeasing I'd been doing was going to get me killed anyway.

"Get in," he said. He wasn't looking like he wanted to take "No" or "Let me think about it" for an answer, and

Peas Passer pushed me off him with more strength than I would have predicted for a guy who never lifted anything heavier than his spoon or his lapels. Part of Todd's hair was standing up, and for some reason I wasn't about to analyze, he had penned a thin black mustache over his upper lip. I was glad Robert Jones was out of sight since Todd clearly didn't need further provocation. One thing you know about a guy when you live with him is when he is in a bad mood. The *chinga-ching* backbeat of "Good Lovin'" rolled out into the fresh late-afternoon air along with the smell of dope and one silver chewing gum wrapper that had been blasted out by the car's defroster.

"Look, man, I'll pay you . . ." I explained, but Todd didn't seem to be listening to or looking for excuses.

I'd seen Todd right after his older brother had given him a wedgie and I'd seen him beat his pillow after his father dressed him down for failing a test on Shakespeare. He had customers that were always trying to get something for free or always frustrated by what he did manage to sell them. He complained about the pressure he was under but he was just like the hockey player. He'd seen a couple of dope dealers on television and thought he knew the scene, waving a gun around in response to the dog-eat-dog rigmarole. I wasn't a dog, or if I was, I was a cocker spaniel or some damn thing that pees on the rug all the time.

"Fuck," said Todd, and I could tell he was stoned, too. "The look on your face."

His laughter at my expense put us on more familiar terms. Because I had chosen not to smoke anything that morning, I felt a craving creep through my lungs. Normally I take a hit off the hookah to wake up and another right before lunch since it brings on the munchies and helps me cope with institutional food. At a deficit of two hits at three-thirty in the afternoon, I was susceptible to hysteria and missing the muddleheaded feeling that made it easier to cope. The music from the two full-size speakers wired into the backseat doppleganged off the administration building, and the car farted one great big pop, which made me think for one completely sickening second that Todd's gun had killed me.

Walt must have thought the same thing because his hands leaped off the lower part of the Camaro's steering wheel and he turned to look at Todd. It took fifteen seconds for me to figure out that I was still intact and that my heart was beating. I checked my shirt for bloodstains and the back of my head for gushing brains without finding them. My life wouldn't have added up to much, but then, who really has the luxury of a life with a purpose? Still, I hadn't been expecting to be killed, and I felt that in the future this might be something I should anticipate and consider in order that it not happen in such a pointless way. Todd also looked down at the barrel of the gun to make sure this hadn't been the source of the noise and then he looked back at me.

"Get in, Beaner," he repeated, a little more reasonably. "We've only got fifteen minutes to make it to the station."

"Wait," I said.

Nobody waited. The members of the hangman team slunk their way back into the fog, looking plenty casual for a bunch of guys who had just seen a guy point a gun at another guy. I wondered why nobody was sending me off with a coat or a pair of socks. I watched them fade away, and then I had this brilliant idea that we could all skip out together, find Robert, pile into Walt's car, and forget our differences. It was the perfect way to thank them for cheering me up and resolving some of my deeper *Star Trek* questions. That's the general idea behind being a Dead Head, to have a "be kind to strangers" outlook and recruit new followers for the church. I realized even before the hangman team was entirely gone, though, that its members were a lousy bunch of cowards, weaseling their way back before finding out whether I was alive, before they had given me the chance to say anything to prove myself a little worthier of the situation, or before I could apologize to Peas Passer for nearly getting him shot first.

"What about Kenny J.?" I leaned into the car and asked Todd.

"*Cats*," Todd said, sneering under his mustache like a guy who really hated cats.

"Who?" I asked.

"*Cats*. He decided to go see *Cats* instead," he shouted over the music. "It was his sister's idea. His mother ordered the tickets."

Todd noticed the look of incomprehension on my face.

"The musical? You know, *Cats*?" he shouted again.

It was hard to believe, and yet there was no explaining Kenny J. Todd lifted his tie-dye shirt—it was my tie-dye shirt—and showed me the sheet of Donald Duck windowpane taped to his chest. He knew I loved the look of a lot of acid in one place. Not only was it just plain colorful, I could feel the stuff working its way from Todd's skin into my nervous system, turning my synapses into color television static. Besides the backpack, the sheet of acid, and the tape in the deck, Todd had brought along a white carton of takeout Chinese food. It sat next to him on the car seat, leaning against the speakers, the wire handles compressed to hold the top closed. Todd must have taken the tape (Oxford Plains, 1988) from my shelf when he packed his gear, along with the recording supplies and drugs he would need at Freedom Coliseum. Since we were roommates, that kind of taking was called borrowing and sharing. If we had not been freaks, it would have been called stealing. Todd had also helped himself to a pair of my favorite dancing skeleton pants and a tie-dye T-shirt while he was at it. Freaks are supposed to have a share-and-share-alike attitude about their possessions, but Todd was only good at part of the equation. He had more of a share-and-sell-alike attitude. The guy was a born capitalist.

"We don't have time for farting around, Beaner," Todd said. He turned to look at the back of Walt's head for confirmation.

"Do we?" he asked Walt.

Walt shook his head no, and I got to thinking that Todd's Snidely Whiplash mustache was overdoing the joke. Poor Walt. He also looked about as scared as a guy could get without coming apart. I wondered what had put Todd in such a lousy mood. Dosing the hall monitor was bad enough, but harassing Walt was just mean. From the look of it, Todd had called on Walt's services at the last minute and had lured him away from his family and their Parents' Weekend activities. They had been having fun together, the littlest Hackett dancing to the string trio's music, Walt and his dad having seconds and thirds of the turkey.

"Put the gun down," I suggested.

Todd stuck his finger in his ear and wiggled it, but without giving me more argument he let the gun rest in his lap. Walt blinked.

For two years, Walt had been our steadiest, most consistent supplier of rides to the train station and to the post office to pick up Todd's packages. We used his father's name on the sign-out sheet when we disappeared at night but had been giving him a break since Halloween, when we'd nearly gotten him in trouble with the headmaster for using his name to sign ourselves out for a whole weekend of shows at the Meadowlands. The tragedy was that Walt was trying to get into MIT. He had already bought all the MIT pens, sweatshirts, car deodorizers, window stickers, book covers, notebooks, and coffee cups a guy would ever want to own. I'd never seen anyone so obsessed by a school with such a serious reputation for turning geeks into bigger geeks. He never once got high with us and spent all his free time (when he wasn't driving us around) at the library, which was a pity, because I'd always thought he was a smart guy, even without the studying, the kind of guy who could use the word *triangulate* without sounding like an asshole.

I gave Walt a wave and a smile, doing my best to make things friendly again and comforting myself with the idea that Todd had meant the gun for Walt instead of me and they had only come upon me accidentally. I picked up my lost sock and wormed into the backseat of the car, almost sitting on the white takeout box with the Chinese food. Something inside slid from one side to the other. Between the two speakers, Todd, Todd's backpack, and me, the backseat was crowded. The door squeaked as I pulled it shut and, almost instantly, mist from our breath covered the back windows. The music in the car was so loud I could feel it in my bones. Empty Cheetos bags lined the floor. Gum wrappers were wedged between the seats, along with a couple of miscellaneous screwdrivers, a banana peel, two copies of *Car and Driver* magazine with the pages spread open and tearing away from the staple, and somebody's old lunch box. I swear to God, I also heard something moving somewhere, a light tapping or rustling coming from the direction of Todd's Chinese takeout box. Todd didn't budge an inch to give me more room. He gestured with the takeout box in the direction of the front seat on the passenger side.

"Move up," he said, holding himself against the seat back, hissing almost. He was so close to me, I could smell the patchouli on his (my) T-shirt and a little bit of carbon burning in the air between us.

I climbed half over Todd and the lunch box and the stick shift and into the front. I accidentally knocked the gun in Todd's lap, and even over the pelvis-grinding thump of "Shakedown Street," I could hear Walt suck in his breath. His jaw contained a hint of green. He held the steering wheel in both hands, and his mouth worked up and down like he was talking to somebody through his teeth. Road trips weren't supposed to start with bad vibes, everybody tense and uptight, a gun pointed at someone else—although, to be honest, a few of them had before this one, minus the gun. I remembered a road trip with my mother and one of my stepfathers in which my mother got out of the car at a rest stop north of Kittery, Maine, and called a cab to take her to the airport. My stepdad at the time, Emerson, went someplace and ate a burger. I sat in the car counting trucks coming down the highway. I got to 132 before I hitched to the airport myself.

You had to be careful how you stepped out for a Dead show. Too much baggage could spoil a trip. It was better to clear your heart so the music could sink in, let bygones be bygones. In order to dispel the mood inside the Camaro, I reached over and punched Walt on the arm. If I could have, I would have told him to lighten up. Instead, Todd leaned between the seats and whispered in Walt's ear.

"Step on it, Hackett," he demanded.

Walt panicked. Without giving me time to fiddle with my seat belt, he slammed the gas pedal hard enough to make the car lurch forward and heave off the curb.

I hit the dashboard and pushed myself back while we sailed through the stop sign at the end of the drive and peeled out down Stillwater Boulevard, the tires of the Camaro squealing, the engine whining. I caught one quick glimpse of the hangman team out the window, near the dorms. Robert Jones was traveling with them, still tucked into Leaky Pen's coat. We went fast enough to pin our heads to the Naugahyde headrests but not fast enough to make Todd drop the gun, which was the plan I think Walt was hoping to enact. Todd reached out and grabbed the back of my seat to hold himself forward, and the car screamed out the front gates of the school into the greater metropolis of Stillwater.

Despite our speed, we couldn't outrun the sadness of the day. The town was still ugly. The Christmas decorations hanging from the light posts shed their glitter onto the road and onto the brown slush along the curb. We went by a dozen empty buildings, the storefronts soaped over, FOR LEASE signs pasted in them. We went by Sam's and Hu Fong's and the Westmarket. The star on a Christmas tree in the park tilted sideways, its twinkle yellow and far away in the fog. Walt didn't bother to slow down when the road started to get slick on the other side of the business district. Just enough people were milling around or coming home from Christmas shopping that our roaring engine caused a few heads to come up and people to back up out of the crosswalks.

I had seen enough car chases on TV to know what Walt, Todd, and I were in for in the next few minutes. A woman would drop her packages and flee to the sidewalk. After missing her, we would skid into and knick a set of vegetable bins, spilling peppers and spreading ripe tomatoes across our windshield. We would have just enough time to breathe a sigh of relief before a pair of construction workers would cross the road with a sheet of glass twenty feet long and ten feet high. Their confusion about which side of the road to run to meant we were going to drive right through the glass and shatter it into a hundred thousand little pieces, causing the tires to blow, traffic to pile up, and one car to drive up over a sand pile and flip three times. After that, it was also only a matter of time before a big black-and-white police cruiser eased up behind us—I knew that was coming, too. I'd seen it happen at least a dozen times to Burt Reynolds, the Dukes of Hazzard, and Chevy Chase.

This was our scene, the end of days and days of staring at chalkboards, ignoring sloppily dressed English instructors who carefully explained iambic pentameter, watching math teachers who clicked the buttons of their ballpoint pens and put them back in their pockets ink end down, staining one good shirt after another. I wondered, as we shot through the fog, if I would miss them. I prayed we would only get busted for dope and reckless driving rather than end up splattered all over the side of some building. Even though the administration had made it policy over the years to ignore our drug abuse, the outside world was a different story. Some state trooper would have been more than happy to put my sorry rich ass in jail. We had been warned enough times by the supermarket cashiers who suspected us of shoplifting and the teenage mothers we cut off in movie lines to know it was only a matter of time before the tables turned and our karma bit us in a soft spot.

I was just sorry that Walt was with us. He didn't deserve our fate. I said his name but he watched the road in front of him and kept the gas pedal depressed, the muscles still working in his jaw. The poor guy thought we were talking about smoking cigarettes the first time we offered him a joint, that's how like a little lamb he was.

"I think we're going too fast," I managed to squeak out.

At the word *fast*, Walt's gas pedal foot underwent a second convulsion, and this time Todd let go of the gun, and it skid into the front seat, where it landed near my freezing and sockless feet. The car veered out onto the Route 8 bypass and opened up on the pavement. One of the promises I made to myself as the world went whipping by was that I would never make fun of domestic automobiles again, the Camaro's fake leather interior and dyspeptic engine, the brown carpeting and MIT deodorizer. The old crate was as solid as a barrel hurtling over Niagara Falls. One of the speakers in the seat next to Todd came loose and pitched forward onto the floor. All kinds of gum wrappers and napkins that had been nesting in the seats fluttered into the atmosphere. I kept hoping we would run out of gas, or the engine would drop off. My life flashed before my eyes—the good parts: the thumb I once sucked, the pony, Jerry. I kept thinking of the slickness of the road and the thinness of the metal that suspended us above it.

Between the two of us, Todd and I tried eighteen positions for crash safety each: hands over our heads, holding on to the seats, bracing our bodies back away from the windshield. Then we tried them all again. I had read somewhere that if you were relaxed or drunk or stoned during a crash, you stood a much better chance of surviving, that your muscles protected your bones with their softness. Just my luck, I was straight for the first time in a hundred years. Tai chi, yoga, meditation, or a fifth of vodka—anything would have come in handy just then. We bounced into the air at the last intersection before the train station. Instead of visions of my child-hood flashing before my eyes, a white-hot sheet of blank paper projected itself, nothing written on it, nothing to declare. Music played from the one speaker that hadn't unplugged. Bobby was telling me that I had to have love. Christ, I wanted to live up to his words. I wanted to be where people were listening to music and not hit the windshield and split like another tomato.

I wouldn't have made it in reform school, although I think Todd would have been OK. Public school was an even worse proposition, since I'd have to live at home to attend one and if you gave me more than one clothing option, I'd blow it every time. I hated to admit it, but maybe Stillwater was a better place for me than I had ever considered. After all, they didn't *really* make me give up my freakishness; they just pretended to. A little hypocrisy was not necessarily a bad thing—what about Jerry and those ties? Walter peeled into a parking lot and hit the brakes; the car spun before it settled. Three times I saw the white Christmas lights on the front of the Stillwater train station blinking through the fog; three times I felt my heart lift and drop itself back into place again. Walter took a deep breath and pounded the steering wheel with his fist.

"Never again," he said.

The train station blazed red and orange and blue behind its front windows. In the fog, the entire town began to wink and blink, as if all of the Christmas lights had been plugged in simultaneously, tie-dyeing the branches of trees and rooftops, splashing the town with neon. Walt pulled his keys from the ignition. Then he began to boil—not just a quiet tirade but a really loud one. I had felt like expressing myself ever since I had been abandoned by the lunch guys, ever since Todd had pulled his gun, and was probably crying somewhere inside but hadn't had enough time to notice. Todd didn't say a word from the backseat. I looked at him in the rearview mirror, saw him still holding the Chinese takeout box between his knees, not looking nearly as shaken up as I was. He smoothed his hair back into place and wiped a little sweat out from underneath his nose, taking some of the Snidely Whiplash mustache away with it. The gun lay like a forgotten toy on the floor of the Camaro.

"You guys are sick," Walter said. "You guys are truly twisted."

I knew what was coming. Walt was a townie, after all, and had grown up with a certain perspective on those of us at the academy. According to Walt, he hadn't been doing anything but eating an innocent lunch and taking an innocent walk to the library before Todd had waylaid him. "You guys just move into a person's life"—Walt got rolling—"and take what you want and move out again. You guys have so much money you think you can do what you want and nobody is going to stop you because your big rich daddies can buy you a big rich lawyer and get you out of it and leave the little guys like me to pay the price. You guys suck pond water. You guys suck cat pee. You guys suck—" Walter had a lot of breath in him, and he kept going on and on about us sucking this and blowing that and how Stillwater High, the public school, could kick our khaki butts and what a bunch of overprivileged jackasses we all were.

How was a guy like Walter, who had a pretty nice family, supposed to know anything about Todd's and my life? Maybe I should have been more satisfied than I was, more adjusted than I was because my stepdad's summerhouse had twenty-seven rooms. If I was spoiled, it was an accident, and I didn't see what it had to do with Walt's troubles. I didn't see how a four-hundred-dollar-a-month allowance, a trust fund, and the second-best music system in the quad made me happier, how it gave me what I wanted—a little peace and quiet, some karmic serenity. Who said you had to have a million dollars to feel good about yourself? Maybe you could afford a better shrink, but that didn't mean you could tell him what he wanted to hear. I knew all there was to know about living a lousy life. I *was* living a lousy life. At this point, it was Freedom or bust. I needed to get among the sane people and I needed Jerry so bad I could have put the gun to Walt's head myself. The windows of the car fogged and I couldn't see a damn thing outside. I kept waiting for Todd to tell Walt to take it easy, but he kept quiet.

"You guys blow elephant dick," Walt said.

Todd slapped him on the back, one, two, three, like they were buddies again, like he was heroically dislodging a piece of food stuck in Walt's throat. Walter's breath heaved in and out of him and he wound down. I eased out, too. Trust was the main tenet of the freak experience. Whatever happened, you just had to go with it, have faith in the big picture, keep on trucking. Walt looked at himself in the rearview mirror. Snot ran down his nose, and big red blotches mixed up with the freckles on his face.

"Wow," he said as if he had stumbled on an existential truth. Hyperventilation can bring on profundity as quick as anything else can.

I dug a McDonald's napkin, only slightly used, out of the glove compartment, blew my own nose, and handed the napkin to him. Walt blew his nose, too, and looked at himself in the mirror again. He looked like my grandmother after plastic surgery—puffy half circles under his eyes and creases around his lips. The tape playing in the deck hissed between songs and started up with "Ramble on Rose." It was just like Jerry to keep singing despite the frenzy. The car was such a mess of junk, we could hardly see our own feet.

"Wow," Walt said again, leaning into the backseat

and inspecting first the speaker and then, when neither Todd nor I replied, the snot on the inside of his crumpled McDonald's napkin. Todd didn't make a move, just tapped the lid of the takeout box between his knees.

He was deciding how to take Walt's outburst. I tried to avoid another vengeance plot. Walt needed to figure out how to make up for what he had just said. I happened to respect Walt. He was nice to people. He'd helped us along, and not because we had tricked him—nobody was that stupid. Two years of free rides and our zero interest in the old people at his volunteer job were enough to indicate we were not on the up-and-up. Maybe we brought something to his life, too, that had nothing to do with going to MIT or being the linchpin of a family or being a success in every damn thing he took up. Revenge gets ugly when you play it on too many people. I had seen my mother sink enough luxury imports to the bottom of our pool after arguments with my steps to know that she never accomplished what she was truly after: a little leverage over someone else's heart.

"Dude," I said, just to say something. "We could all use a little dope after that ride." It was a hint for Todd to show mercy and, maybe, in the meantime, extend me some credit. I seriously hoped that Todd knew he had kidnapped a broke man.

He met my eyes in the reflection of the rearview mirror. I couldn't tell what was rattling around inside. He was as blank and about as unreadable as a novel by Charles Dickens.

"What do you say?" I asked.

But he didn't answer. Something besides Walter's words seemed to be occupying him and something about Walt's tirade had made him come to a decision. He began to gather up his stuff, pushing the back of my seat ahead to get out the door. Walt looked like he had one more thing to say before we left. We had never asked Walt to come along to a show, and he had never asked to join us. I had been telling Walt for months how Jerry was the magic answer to just about everything and how beautiful the music could be. All he would have to do was call from New York or somewhere and tell his parents that he would be working late at the library. Todd hummed a little "Ramble on Rose" along with Jerry, reached into the open car door, pulled his backpack and the Chinese takeout box from the backseat, and then told Walt to come along. I didn't see whether he had put the gun away in the pack with his other things or stashed it under the seat to retrieve on the ride home. I hoped it was still in the car. I didn't want to deal with it at Freedom. I didn't want to deal with it ever.

"The gun wasn't loaded," I told Walt when Todd was out of earshot.

Walt looked at me, confused.

"No bullets," I said again.

Walt got a look on his face. I'd seen the look, but never on Walt—sort of a bunched-eyebrows kind of look. People made it when something smelled bad.

"I know," he lied.

He wasn't the only one faking it. I had no idea whether the gun was loaded. I just couldn't stand the thought of Walt, who had been so pure in the past, getting a whiff of how tainted we were, thinking we were criminals. He jumped out of the Camaro and slammed the door, trucking after Todd up the concrete steps to the train platform, leaving me sitting alone in the car. I pulled my still-wet socks out of my pocket, smelled them, and decided they were better off in my coat since they would only add to the chafe on my ankles. Something wasn't quite right about Walt making his way across the parking lot after Todd. We only had two tickets to the show, which was sold out, and Walt was too inexperienced to deal with scalpers. The mood created by the gun hadn't quite lifted, and I felt some reckoning still hovering in the air, the triangle of friendship not quite made equilateral by the new Walt, the sneering Walt, the truth-telling, won't-be-pushed-around Walt, the Walt who was coming because Todd had invited him. I headed up the platform, making sure the Camaro was locked up first, although I didn't know who the hell would want to steal it—there's not much of a market for Naugahyde interiors these days, and besides, the car sucked.

CASEY JONES

TODD AND I traditionally packed a couple of backpacks before we went to a show. He carried the necessary stuff like tickets, recording equipment, and warm clothes in case it rained. Sometimes he carried money and a little dope should we get separated, especially if we were planning to trip hard and burn out our faculties in such a way that might make recognizing each other difficult. I brought along entertainment—a Walkman, some tapes, acid, video games, a Hacky Sack if I was really desperate, Frisbees, and kids toys (one time LEGOs and another time one of those electric helicopters that attached to a wire and was piloted with a remote control). I also brought along reading material: comic books and copies of *High Times,* and the *Highlights* that I ripped off from dentists' offices. "Goofus and Gallant" was a great way to pass the minutes when I was getting ready to trip hard—that Goofus is a riot. We also brought stuff to trade—drugs, tie-dye shirts, copies of tapes, tickets to other shows. I mostly carried the contraband in my pack, leaving Todd's hands free to make transactions.

We argued about me being the vulnerable one, but it was like Robin arguing with Batman. It was the ward's job to attract trouble so that the superhero could deflect it. But it was not just getting busted by security that made me squirrelly; it was the customers themselves who could be off center, always paranoid about what you were selling them or what you might cut things with. Todd and I tried to arrive early to give ourselves time to play, do business, and duct-tape what we were bringing into the show under our clothes. Duct tape is an essential item, one that Todd carried in his pack.

Other Dead Heads had their own methods for bringing in contraband. They stashed joints in their dreadlocks, flasks under their plaid shirts, and dugouts in their socks. Instead of sporting the usual Birkenstocks, some freaks wore shoes that had stowage in the toes. There was no manual for bringing a gun into the show, probably because taping posed a problem and holsters were a risky accessory. I kept hoping Todd had ditched his gun in the car. Without a backpack of my own, I was traveling light, but not so light I didn't think I could make it. Todd stopped inside the doors of the station and pulled me away from the ten or twenty people doing whatever the hell it was people did in train stations.

"So about the g-u—?" I whispered.

"The men's room," Todd said.

Walter followed us into the bathroom, where instead of answering my question Todd told me he wanted to switch out the acid. We went back into one of the bathroom stalls, and once we had the door shut behind us, he lifted his shirt and pulled at the tape on his chest, trying not to get it tangled in the cellophane that encased the tabs. I helped when it looked like it was going to tear.

"Easy, Beaner," Todd said, wincing.

Except for Walt, we were alone, which was lucky considering a stranger might have made the wrong assumption about what we were up to, two guys in a bathroom stall asking each other to be gentle.

"So about the gun?" I asked again.

"Don't worry about it, Beaner," Todd said.

I was going to ask him why not, but Todd suddenly winced again. He didn't have any more chest hair than I did, mostly as a result of all those days when he traveled solo, but even so, the tape took its time peeling off. Once we had it, he worked to reapply the sheet to me using the same sections of tape that had been sticking to him. I backed up against the toilet, trying not to fall in while Todd flattened out the sheet. Walt, meanwhile, used the urinal and washed his hands. I think he was avoiding knowing what we were up to, being an accessory to our crime. Todd gave him a smile when we came out but didn't say anything about him still being with us. Once we were finished with the transfer, we left the men's room and crossed the waiting area to the ticket booths.

Todd approached the counter first, and the guy behind the desk snapped, "Where to and how many?" Todd told him one to Grand Central. The clerk took Todd's five-spot, flicked back the change with his thumb, and then asked Walt how many and where to. Walt also said one. The clerk was good at watching the money and not making eye contact, likely the reason he hadn't come in one morning to find he had been replaced by a vending machine. I wondered whether his flicking thumb ever got sore. I liked how he flicked, though. In the words of Kenny J., "It was cool."

When it was my turn, I approached the counter, and the guy asked me where to and how many, and I answered before I checked my pants' pockets. There was lint in there, an old movie ticket, something that must have been a breath mint once, and a fuzzy nickel. I tried the pockets on my handshaker suit and came up with an extra button and some bread from the dining hall. Finally I checked the pockets of my peacoat, where I found my wet socks. Everybody took a step back when those came out, so I put them away again and kept looking. Todd noticed that I was coming up empty at about the same time Walt did and muttered something under his breath.

Todd was always on me about money, and it was true I turned up with either too much or not enough in all the wrong places, and that I owed him two hundred twenty dollars. I almost got us mugged once by pulling out a wad of fifties to tip a shoeshine guy, and we had to dine and ditch at more than one restaurant in our travels because I had forgotten it was my turn to treat. By this time, the guy at the counter noticed I wasn't paying him for the ticket he had printed and pinned under his middle and index fingers. There was an awkward pause in which everyone shifted their weight across their feet—Todd and Walt because I was making them look bad, the three people behind me because they were pricks, and the old guy at the counter because he was going to have to void the ticket if I didn't pony up.

"Can I borrow five bucks?" I asked Todd, hoping that he might remember that it was him who had made me leave at gunpoint without the usual supplies.

Walt dug a crumpled fiver out of his pocket and handed it through the window. Otherwise Todd would have left me right there, still digging. There was a line Todd drew when it came to freeloaders, and I was drawing damn close to it. The guy released the ticket and flicked back a dollar and a quarter, the correct change for a child under ten. What the heck would a ten-year-old kid be doing traveling with two teenagers? It wasn't like Todd, Walt, and I looked like brothers. It was the goddamned hand-shaker suit that made me look so young. Stick a tie on a guy whose neck has not matured and it makes people instantly think of bibs. Instead of correcting his mistake, I took the extra buck and spent it on some Cheetos from the vending machine.

That's another thing that goes in the backpack: food, a ready supply of Ding Dongs and Ho Hos. Todd had made a tidy business out of selling snacks at twice the price to freaks with the munchies. The Westmarket where we shopped before a show was a sorry replacement for the Grand Union on the other end of town, but we ended up there most of the time because it was within walking distance of the station and because the checkout people tended not to notice when we swiped from the candy shelves. Whoever owned the Westmarket kept milk in the cooler a week past the expiration date, and the linoleum on the floor had chips missing and gummy stuff exposed, which made pushing a cart through the aisles like taking a mountain pass into the Andes. The only advantage to the Westmarket that I could see was that the women who worked the counter were too drunk or tired to reslide stuff over the bar scanner when they missed or to notice when packs of M&Ms went missing, so sometimes we got a discount. At the Grand Union, they've got teenage corporate Nazis in clip-on bow ties working checkout, which means the only discounts are legal ones.

After I'd fetched my Cheetos from the machine, I went out onto the platform after Todd and Walt. They had found themselves a bench and Walt was talking while Todd tilted toward him suddenly buddy-buddy. Todd was a different guy from the one who had been delivering a lecture on Klingons twenty-four hours earlier. He was suddenly receptive, and I could tell he was listening. Walt shut up as I got close and it pissed me off. It made no sense given the lousy things Walt had said in the Camaro and Todd's performance with the gun, which had wigged out Walt as much as it had me no matter what he pretended. I reached out with the bag of Cheetos and asked them if they wanted any.

"No thanks," they said together. I noticed Todd still had his Chinese takeout box and figured that was why he wasn't hungry.

Instead of joining them, I dug into the bag of Cheetos for a mouthful of cheesy deliciousness and wiped the orange dust on my blue jacket. I was really missing my freak clothes, the T-shirt Todd had borrowed without asking. I didn't think I stood a chance of getting it back before we got to Freedom. Before I could ask Todd if there were any other clothes I could borrow from the pack, a whistle blew and a train burned by going north on the opposite tracks. Todd bundled up in my Guatemalan sweater. He blew on his fingers, looked at his watch, tapped his takeout box, and shoved his hands in his pockets, pulling out pieces of lint and dropping them onto the platform, where they fluttered and landed near his feet. Walter sat quietly by him, looking at his hands. If it were me, I'd be asking all kinds of things: How long is it going to take us to get there? How are we going to get home again? What will happen if we get caught? Poor Walt. He was too damn trusting by half.

I finished the Cheetos and walked up the platform to toss the empty bag in the trash. As I was coming back, I brushed by a woman with a toddler in her arms. Even after I passed her I felt her watch me. I knew the look I was getting: It was an "aren't you one of those rich kids from that school" look. The women in the Westmarket, the movie theater, and the mall stared the same way. I tried feigning innocence but it was a major handicap wearing the handshaker suit, and with no socks I was easily flagged as an asshole preppie. I thought about waiting for her and telling her that someone in my family had died. I'm not even sure I would have worn a suit to a funeral, I hated suits so much. I felt like a guy out selling insurance or running for president; I felt like I was going to bid on stocks at any second.

Todd looked up and watched. The woman began following me, but she had trouble maneuvering while she balanced her kid. Todd picked up his pack and the take-out box from the bench and yanked Walter down the platform. Suddenly I realized what Todd was realizing, that the woman was getting close.

"Excuse me." She grabbed me by the elbow.

The platform was crowded with people on their way into the city, and she must have had to do some slaloming to get to me so fast. She was young but, even so, hard like the women working in the dining hall, wearing black leather half boots and earrings the size and shape of Ferris wheels. I could see the will to do me harm in her eyes. I was going to beg for mercy, blurt out the truth about where we were going and what we were up to, offer her money—anything. Her kid tried to crawl out of her arms and take a swan dive onto the pavement between us. He had so much red hair that his head resembled an eraser.

"Aren't you one of those snobbies from up at the school?" the woman asked.

I nodded and, I'm sorry to say, I swallowed.

"Aren't you going to get in trouble for sneaking out?"

"I have permission," I lied, and watched her eyes get narrower.

"Those must be your friends up the way."

I looked down the platform at Walt and Todd. Walt was watching but pretending not to. Todd was staring down at the ground.

"No . . . who? . . . I don't know what you're talking about," I said.

"Uh-huh." She freed her son and crossed her arms.

Enjoying his parole, the kid ran up and down the concrete platform, threatening to toss himself onto the third rail. The woman hardly moved to check. I could tell she was inspecting the buttons on my blazer, trying to decide for herself if they were real gold, and laughing inwardly about the school insignia on the breast pocket. Stillwater has a coat of arms: a couple of ducks on a pond surrounded by cattails, or something that looks like cattails. I tried to get my peacoat closed, but it was too late. I wished that I had taken off my damn tie. There was no reason for me to be wearing a tie. I would have shoved it in my pocket as soon as I had left the dining hall but my socks were already there and there are only so many arti-cles of clothing you can stuff into the pocket of a peacoat. I gave some thought to bumping her onto the tracks but didn't have the heart, what with her having a small child. I was about to give myself up when a guy crowded to the white line and leaned out to look down the tracks.

"I think I see the train," he said to no one in particu-lar. Immediately people arose from their metal benches. The kid got knocked over and began to yowl.

By the time the woman had gathered Junior in her arms, I had gotten myself into the rush and another twenty feet down the platform. The regular riders had the inside information, knowing ahead of time where the engineer was going to put on the brakes and the doors were going to open. Fortunately, there were far fewer of them on a Saturday afternoon. As the cars glided for-ward I glimpsed the people already inside as they read or worked on crossword puzzles in their seats. No freaks that I could tell. Some guy Knees' age looked back at me—probably thinking daydreamy thoughts and letting the metronome of clackety-clack lull him into a stupor. You get a strong sense that the people in the windows have homes and places to go and things that they love when you see them framed like that. I always felt rushed away by an approaching train, blurred like a piece of white lint floating in the evening air.

The train shrieked and stopped with a door right in front of me. Todd and Walt hooked in behind me and we found three empty places facing three other empty seats in the second car we passed through. I sat down hard and Todd and Walt took the seats that faced me. Before the train started to move again, I looked out the window toward the platform and spotted the woman holding on to her kid by the hood of his coat and waving down some dude with a shaved head who had gotten off the train farther up. She seemed small from my vantage point and I thought it was sweet that she had spent all that time waiting instead of going, though it wasn't sweet that she had killed the minutes by harassing me. For a second I imagined being married to her and raising her redheaded kid. The train lurched and then sped up, and she was gone. I looked out the window and then at Todd in the opposite seat.

"Jesus, Beaner," Todd said when he saw my look.

He slipped on his Walkman headphones, and the train picked up speed. We stopped a few minutes later at the Westport station, where seven or eight more people entered our car. Walt had to slide in closer to Todd and I had to sit up to make room for a couple of older women with white hair and pearls who were too lazy to walk more than five feet before sitting down. They worked their way out of their fur coats while they kept up a happy chat about their grandsons and laid the coats in the empty seat on the aisle as a barrier against the other passengers still coming through the doors.

I wasn't too thrilled to be sharing our space with Barbara Bush, her friend, Barbara Bush Two, and what must have been a thousand pounds of happy, frolicking minks only a few months ago. I was seriously thirsty after the Cheetos and sleepy from all the hangman activity and wanted to stretch out. Walt gave the two Barbaras a friendly smile, the kind of smile that made him seem like such a patsy, and pulled out a book from the inside pocket of his coat—a science-fiction number with a gorilla girl on the cover. He didn't explain what he was still doing with us or how he was going to score his own ticket; instead, he kept tagging along in that quiet way of his. It made his presence seem like a coincidence, like he was on the train by mistake, had just happened to see us here and

144

wasn't really a part of our group. I wondered what words were going by in that book of his to make him so silent and sure of himself.

"Whatcha reading, Walt?" I asked him.

He tilted the cover so I could read the title, something about an invasion of gorilla people on a gorilla world. I looked at the cover art more than the words and decided that despite his constant friendliness, the five bucks he had loaned me, and the volunteer work he did, he was a jerk. Barbara Bush and her friend in the seat next to Todd looked like they were itching to make a grandmotherly stab at conversation. Women that age dig younger men in ties and guys like Walt who smiled at them, but Walt was as good as dead, his eyes slipping back and forth across the page, taking in some fascinating otherworldly encounter that involved semidressed, ultramuscular gorillas with ray guns.

"Are you boys on a field trip?" the Barbara next to Todd asked me. She directed her question my way since she didn't stand a chance with Walt, and Todd had on his headphones. I acted surprised that she was talking to me.

"What?" I asked.

"Are you boys on a field trip?" the woman repeated, less nicely this time, more like she was another one who wanted to run us in for truancy.

Walt looked up and then back down again. As a scholarship student, he was the most likely to face life-changing repercussions if we were caught. The administration at Stillwater had a policy of coming down on guys like him faster and harder than they came down on paying guys like Todd and me. At Stillwater, Todd and I had been busted for just about everything, all the minor stuff besides Haley the goldfish—tardiness, messiness, low grades, and lewdness. Once, Todd and I had even been busted for art theft. During one of our more creative phases, Kenny J. and Todd and I had borrowed a Smithsonian reproduction of a Fabergé egg from the proctor's office, took it up to our room for three or four hours, and swapped turns sitting on it. We had built a nest out of a couple of Todd's pillows and my dirty gym socks, convinced by the power of our imaginations and a hit of acid apiece that a Fabergé chicken was going to pop out.

The proctor issued an all-points bulletin for the "misguided individual or individuals" who had invaded his premises. The announcement gave the usual two hours for the culprit(s) to come forward before losing sign-out privileges. By then, Kenny J. and I had decided to cook and eat the egg instead, but Todd wanted to make a deal with someone, trade for an eighth with his brother or sell on the open market. We were bored at the time, and the chicken thing had seemed like a worthwhile excursion into the weird to keep ourselves busy—better than counting the number of times Kenny J. said "cool" in an afternoon and better than doing our geometry homework. Of course, we got caught. We accidentally left the egg in one of my shoes in the common area. My stepfather donated some money—probably enough to buy a new trinket for the proctor and a library—and that combined with what Todd's and Kenny's parents kicked in settled everybody down. All Walt had to do was sneeze too loudly and he would have found himself hauled out of Stillwater by the seat of his pants and deposited outside the gates. It was an ugly, fucked-up system, one that meant Walt had a responsibility to help me throw the ladies off his scent.

"We're going to the New York Public Library," I explained. "We're going to write a report."

"How nice." The woman smiled.

"On what?" the other woman inquired, patting her pearls.

I tried to think. Todd was the one who had the good head for details, but he was not acting his usual glib self and charming the old bats into submission. I was more of an abstract thinker—a definite limitation for a person who had to come up with frequent alibis. I wiped a hole in the mist on the window and glanced outside, watching the streets that bordered the tracks. The train slowed, and we passed a Volvo stopped at an intersection, the backseat loaded with kids on their way to some lesson, maybe hockey or horseback riding or trombone.

"Capitalism," I said, watching the Volvo.

The Barbaras shifted around and clutched their purses as if any talk about money made them nervous.

"What about capitalism?" one of them asked—the truant officer, the one who seemed to be the bossier and nosier of the two.

"How it works," I said.

I had no idea whether I had been specific enough or convincing enough to throw her off my trail. Still, she and her friend were silent for a while, formulating their next question. It's darn tricky turning capitalism into small talk, and the challenge slowed them down. The train came to a stop at the South Norwalk station, and a woman carrying a six-month-old baby waddled into our car looking for a seat. The South Norwalk station is a lot less brightly lit than the Westport one and there was a ruffling of papers as conversation in the car ceased. I could sense people pulling the cord on their personal space, inflating it the way you do survival suits on sinking boats. The woman with the baby used her other arm to lug along a dirty shopping bag full of sour-milk and dirty-diaper smells. She went down the car once and came back, the bag whacking the seats and people's elbows and shoulders as she passed. When she reached us a second time, she paused at the sight of the minks. The old ladies glanced at each other, the one opposite me arching an eyebrow at her friend. I watched a debate unfold between them eyebrow by eyebrow. The train lurched and the baby's mother took matters into her own hands.

"Move in," she said, as if she understood how hard it was for the Barbara Bushes to show some Christian charity.

The older ladies sighed and collected their fur coats into their laps. The woman with the baby came heaving down, bag and all, in one great big thump. She ran a hand through her limp black hair and set the baby on one knee, making an attempt to pull down its pajama shirt and pull up its pants, but it didn't work, and the baby squirmed and untucked everything, exposing a grape juice stain next to its belly button. The woman lowered her eyelids. I think she was letting us know that sitting with us was going to be a chore for her, too. She reminded me of the troubled mothers of the teenage homosexuals on *Bunny*, her face saggy, her free arm hanging heavily over the side of the seat like it had weights in the fingers. She seemed to be searching for an answer to a problem too complicated to be expressed. The baby, on the other hand, was wild for attention. It contorted itself in its mother's arms and spit its pacifier out of its mouth, bouncing it off its mother's knee onto the floor. Four heads collided at once—the brushy head of the old lady nearer me, her friend's, Walt's, and mine. Everyone except Todd and the mother made a grab for the escaping pacifier.

"Here it is." The nicer of the two old ladies waved it.

That kid didn't hesitate. It took one look at that smiling old lady holding out its pacifier and screamed until its face turned purple. The kid's mother accepted it from the old lady and, despite the lint sticking to it, replugged the kid's mouth before we all went deaf. Todd got up, excused himself, and left the car. He was either headed to the restroom or to the bar car for a drink. "Restroom" was what he said as he tripped over the woman's baby bag, but I guessed otherwise. I only hoped he would bring something back for me with him. The kid's mother gave Todd's (my) tie-dye a dirty look as he passed. She had already given my suit and tie and the old ladies' fur coats a dirty look. It seemed to me that she had something against clothes in general.

"We're going to the Dead show in Freedom," I said, forgetting what I had just told the old ladies, feeling like I had to rap with her because the insulation that surrounded her was thin.

If you don't have money, you can't pretend as easily that you are better than other people. The two Barbaras were the type to notice the woman's greasy hair and smelly baby, the type to infer that she ought to go find herself a job and clean herself up, but if they were anything like my grandmother, they hadn't worked a day in their lives either, unless you call driving a golf cart work. While I watched for signs that the mother was going to lash out, she shifted her baby to her other knee and stared at it for a minute. Her face was as expressionless as if she were looking at an apple or a rock or another inanimate object of no particular origin. The baby grabbed at her nose, and she jerked it back away from her. The Barbara Bushes patted their pearls.

The train slowed to a stop at Stamford, and a few people got off and more people got on. When we started forward again, I began to wonder where Todd had disappeared to. The mood in the car changed with the Stamford boarders from dull silence to festive anticipation. The off-to-the-city-for-a-party traffic was making itself known, people yelling back and forth to each other from their scattered seats. A Santa Claus with a dirty beard slept through the noise, his face pressed up against the window glass, his mouth open.

"Where do you think Todd is?" I finally asked Walt.

He looked up from his book and checked around like he was noticing for the first time that Todd was gone.

"Want me to look for him?" he asked, but before I could answer, the baby began to wail and no amount of pacifier plugging seemed to help.

We rode along a few minutes longer, listening to

the racket until the mother buried the baby's face in her chest. The old woman next to Walt pointed over my head toward the rear doors and said, "Say, isn't that . . . ," not finishing her sentence. Both the Barbara Bushes and the mother on my side turned to look. Walt rested his book on his lap and looked up, too. I glanced over my shoulder in the direction of the old woman's finger, and felt a jolt of recognition at spying some asshole who had been hanging around our house flirting with my mother a couple of years earlier. All three women sucked in their breath in unison. "It is. I think it is . . . ," they said together. The face of the young woman brightened with more feeling than she had expressed in all her minutes on the train up to that point. She reached over and held on to the arm of the Barbara next to her in an effort to contain herself. The older woman seemed to forget to mind.

Todd came bursting back in from the bar car, and in his hand he held a plastic glass empty of everything except a squeezed slice of lime and three half-melted ice cubes. The Walkman headphones were ringing his neck and I could hear the tape in the deck, Oxford Plains still, faint and small, but reminding me of all that was waiting for me once we got off the train. Todd had a glow like he had been able to score from the bartender not once, not twice, but four or five times. The bartender must have accepted the fake identification Todd flashed him even though it came from a mail-order outfit advertising in the back of some magazine. I imagined Todd standing there, swaying with the car and handing over a couple of fivers, pointing out the Beefeater bottle up on the top shelf.

"You'll never guess who's here, Beaner," he said, tripping over the baby bag on the floor.

"Don't say it out loud." I slunk down.

"He went back into the other car," one of the disappointed older ladies said, her neck craned at a dangerous angle.

"Oh, I just love him," the woman with the baby stated, turning the kid around so that it sat on her lap facing away from her. "I love him."

The baby seemed to be stunned by the news that his mother loved anybody and gave its pacifier an audible tug. There was a lot of jabbering, everybody recognizing my mother's ex-lover, a semicelebrity who acted on *Days of Our Lives* or *Santa Barbara* or some other damn show. The guy made the rounds, and had hung with my mother, just another guy who had had it all but deserved it the least. Guys like him were like monsters in Greek myths—you cut off the head of one and another would pop out in its place. There weren't too many almost-famous men in America who hadn't dated my mother, except Phil Lesh or Mickey Hart. Why those guys hadn't was just my rotten luck. I hated being reminded that even this far away from Stillwater, she could still find a way to mess me up.

I bet the dude had been riding the train for a week in the hopes of being recognized by someone. That's how big an ego the jackass had.

The two Barbara Bushes relived every plotline, every imbecile scene of every soap the guy was ever in while the younger woman and Todd tossed a few things into the mix. It turned out that Dr. Peck Greenfield, aka Boris Ferber, aka Mr. Jackass, all-around asshole, brain surgeon, plane crash survivor, and true father of his long-lost brother's son, had an evil twin, but the revelation must not have done too much for his show's ratings because the character was recently iced in a terrible boating accident. It was too bad that the boating accident hadn't wiped his alter ego, too. After one of his dates with my mother, I walked in on him shaking his johnson over the toilet in our cabana. He strutted around the house in his bikini underwear like he wanted someone to notice that he had just gotten some; when he caught sight of me, he called me Junior and tried to give me a high five.

"He has the widest shoulders," claimed one of the Barbara Bushes.

"I hear he got a movie contract," Walt said.

"He has a quarter-sized wart on his prick," I intervened, halting the stream of chitchat that had begun to flow and join in the car around me.

Everyone turned my way—the old ladies with looks of real concern, the mother and the kid with identical smirks (who knew a baby could smirk?), and Walt and Todd with smiles. I had nothing more to add to the conversation. I had just wanted to save them all from being swept away by their own misguided fantasies. The shapes and shadows of southern Connecticut whipped by outside the train window, and, after a while, the conversation restarted, excluding me.

Sometime between when we had been standing on the platform and when we had gotten on the train, the sun had gone down and, with the fog, closed off the outside world into near total darkness so that the inside of the car was mirrored back at us, a parallel universe an arm's reach away. When he wasn't talking, Todd tapped on his take-out box. Walt put his book away and whistled to himself speculatively. The stations passed by with curved street-lights arching over the tracks and posters for the latest in Broadway musicals.

As we went south, the swimming pools and back-yards were replaced by stripped automobiles and spray-painted bridges, and the tracks and tunnels got darker and dirtier, less like the pristine commuter towns we had come through in the north. The train was going faster, too, not stopping through sections of the Bronx like an outsider afraid of getting mugged. The Barbaras dropped their voices to a whisper. We all ignored a car burning in a parking lot behind a housing project. The baby fell asleep. Todd dug the train schedule to Long Island out of his backpack.

Those who were riding the train with us instead of having dinner with their families were a sorry lot, not a sugarplum still dancing in a single head. Santa slept with his beard gaping open at his chin. I supposed being Santa two weeks before Christmas was the double shift of a life-time. This Santa had soot on the white rims of his sleeves and holes in the toes of his boots. I wondered if he was a homeless Santa or on the lam like we were. We dipped underground at the edge of the city, and for a while I felt like we weren't getting anywhere, just traveling through black empty space, only imagining we were moving.

Once, my mother took me to Macy's so I could meet the real Santa. It made her feel better to know that I believed in something. The guy put me up on his knee and started in with the usual naughty/nice rigmarole until we left it that I would get off his lap and let the next kid in line through. There were about a thousand kids waiting that day, his legs were tired, and I asked a lot of questions. The sad part is that up until that moment, I believed in him, the rat bastard. He was every kid's fat, jolly precursor to Jerry with a bunch of flying reindeer to jazz up the image. I was thankful that I had grown up and it was Jerry who was waiting for me at Freedom. Santa—at least the Santa in our car—appeared to be sleeping off one hell of a bender.

HELL IN A
BUCKET

OTHER EMPTY THOUGHTS rattled my brain and I occupied myself for the last few minutes of our train journey as best I could by trying to pull them all together and buckle them down. Todd composed a symphony, tapping the end of his pencil on his takeout box. I stared and stared at a poster of a bear selling fabric softener. The poster was above Walt's head, on the wall of the car and next to the cigarette ad. The bear was wearing a cute little bow around his neck, and he smiled and waved one of his cute paws. Though the bears on all Jerry's posters and bumper stickers were equally smiley, they never oversold their friendliness. They never seemed as if they were secretly plotting to smother me in my sleep or set fire to my house the way the fabric softener bear seemed to. Having to be so damned cute all the time could have strained anyone's mood. My happiness was stretched thin, too, and I felt like I might snap if I didn't get some kind of break from the darkness of the tunnel.

Finally we reached Grand Central Terminal and rolled under the first bank of fluorescent lights. I felt so tense I hardly knew myself. I imagined the look-alikes of my step-father Knees, guys in suits and ties, carrying briefcases and patting their thinning hair, huddled on the platform every weekday waiting for the train to stop. A person had to be careful not to lose his soul in Grand Central and turn into a commuter zombie, hovering around like an extra for a Hollywood horror movie. The majority of the terminal is underground, with passages winding out into nearly every basement in the city. My mother, afraid of the gloom, took cabs, staying aboveground as much as possible, but there were still car tunnels and the Bronx and restaurants with bathrooms in the sublevel waiting to suck a person in.

"Wake up, Walt," I said, kicking at Walt's left foot.

Walt's choice to follow us to Freedom still baffled me,

and I had spent some of the last minutes of the ride trying to figure him out. It was typical for him to put up a fight on some issues and to give right in and do as he was told on others. But on decisions that determined his future, he nearly always held firm. He was disciplined, for example, when it came to math class, though we made efforts to distract him, get him to blow off homework, or let us use his answers to cheat on tests. I had had two sections of math with Walt when I was a freshman, and I knew he was a genius when it came to numbers. Even if cutting school for Freedom got him kicked out, he'd go on and invent something like the solar microchip or paint-by-googolplex kits or some damn thing. Still, I wondered, as I kicked him awake, why he wasn't in a worse state of remorse over his affairs. He yawned, shrugged, and stood up, like suddenly one destination was just as fine with him as another.

"Only another hour and another train and we'll be there," I told him, but it was more like I was telling myself, reassuring myself that we were still headed for Freedom.

When the train stopped, the Barbara Bush–alikes teamed up to impede our progress toward the doors and out onto the platform. While they fussed, I noticed the baby and his mother were clearing a wedge through the door on the opposite side of the car, the same way they had cleared the way when they had gotten on the train. Their wake was my best bet for escape as long as I avoided the baby's clutches. Todd and Walt gave up on overtaking the Bush–alikes and dropped behind me. Out on the platform, we maneuvered around people on their way to board the train. An event must have finished in town, the Rockettes dancing *The Nutcracker* or some damn thing. Either that or people were drifting north to Connecticut to peep at a few dead leaves. A banker type tossed his old newspaper into a large metal bin. On the other side of the bin, a guy with a ripped army jacket pulled the paper back out, reassembled it, and sold it to an elderly couple going in the other direction for a dollar.

"Newspapers!" the guy with the ripped jacket yelled. "Newspapers!"

"How much do you figure that guy is making?" Todd asked.

Walt did the math. "A lot," he said.

We stood admiring the homeless guy's salesmanship and the wad of cash in his fist, which would have been even bigger on a weekday. I wondered how he was going to spend the money given that household goods—Persian rugs, antique candelabras, a new dining room table—were out of the question. My stepfathers tended to spend cash on cars or, in some cases, summerhouses and sailboats. My own personal form of consumerism took an experiential form: movies, tapes, concert tickets, and acid. Todd humped it up the platform before I could ask the guy and satisfy my curiosity. He moved much too fast for Walt, who was unused to the ruthless ways of the city and bumped elbows with an old lady who he stopped to apologize to. But man, once you start apologizing, you've got to keep apologizing, and it's much easier just to forget the whole ritual and go.

We stuck to the edge alongside the train. Up at the front of the platform, under a sign advertising air travel prices, something glinted in the darkness. A man's gesture, an arm rolling toward a chest, a Rolex on a wrist catching the fluorescent light from the gate.

That flash was like a bomb going off in my head.

"Knees . . . " I began, without really being sure of what I had seen.

Dark places had caused a dark thing to happen to my mind. Laugh and the world laughs with you, I thought.

Everyone loves a lover. Shine on your love light. But I was like a teddy bear with too much optimism in my beady eyes. Todd saw me panic, saw me point up the platform to the place underneath the sign. He shot across the top of the tunnel into the dark, skipping into a side passage that led to the crosstown shuttle. Walt and I hustled to keep up with him. It would have been impossible for me to have met Knees' eyes, let alone his understanding. The treatment would have been a gentle guy-to-guy, this-is-not-the-correct-way-to-handle-your-problems-son discipline. If I had to face him, I was only hoping that it would come after the show, after the fortification of sunshine and daydreams. The hangman team had probably tipped off the headmaster, who had probably been on the phone to my mother, who would have called Knees, and here we all were—or here I thought we all were. Just before we made the exit, I looked back. The man with the Rolex was not where I had seen him, the glint a slippery crescent that had disappeared before my eyes.

And yet somehow I knew he was out there. Without me knowing it, he had always been out there, looking for me, thinking up ways to shape and mold me and turn me into something that belonged to him. We had left some things unsaid at the lunch counter at Sam's, and it was those unspoken words that had been eating at me these few weeks. Todd, Walt, and I hurried through the tunnel, shimmied around a woman with a set of bags open on the floor, and climbed a set of stairs. Walter clung to both of us. In that silent way of his, I think he even managed to steer a little. Todd opened a door marked MEN in the tiled wall of the tunnel and dragged us all out of the semidarkness and into a room lit with flickering ceiling lights so white they looked purple.

"Oh, man," I said.

"This place stinks," Walt said as he cupped his hand over his nose. Then, after our eyes had adjusted, he asked, "Where are we?" He thought about it for a minute. Then he asked, "Is there something wrong with Loveletter's legs?"

"Beaner's?" Todd asked.

"Yes, his legs." Walt pointed at me.

"Knees," Todd explained.

"His knees?" Walt asked.

The question hung in the air. We were alone except for a man curled up on a set of flattened cardboard boxes, a chewed-up white Styrofoam cup perched by his elbow.

The smell in the bathroom didn't seem to waft from the guy on the boxes directly, but it did seem to be a part of him, the way Stillwater had become a part of me or Todd, something people always managed to know about us even when we weren't wearing the uniforms. Mold crept up two of the five stall doors still hanging on their hinges. A toilet must have leaked or overflowed because the floor was wet, littered with paper that had curled over and been stained with several tidemarks. The guy on the floor slept with his face turned into the orange lining of his coat. He twitched like a dog, his fingers rippling and his spine convulsing. He looked well-enough fed, able, but taken down so that he wasn't going to bother trying to do anything but take a nap. And why not? There was something perfectly honest about giving up, slipping off the tight coil of all the stupid hard choices he had to make every day. I felt like lying down next to him, curling up in my peacoat and closing my eyes. Could I have been more of a fuck-up, more of a liability?

"Hell," Todd said, more like he was saying "What the hell" instead of naming the place we had descended to.

I imagined the circumstances that had led the guy on the floor to hole up here. I admit that I was creeped out by the spray-painted mirrors, the fluorescent lights that only half worked, the broken urinal that leaked a rusty puddle of water around its edge, and the metal trash bins that overflowed with paper towels, crushed cigarettes, and two long strands of someone's hair. A half-empty can of Diet Coke trickled into the sink, the black stuff winding down the drain like a snake hunting for mice. The tiles around us on all four sides initially looked bright under the lights but under closer examination revealed years of accumulated grime and the thin gray wisps of cobwebs. A speaker in the corner played Muzak, a tinny, static-filled version of "Bridge over Troubled Water."

"What did you see?" Todd asked.

"I need dope," I said.

The legs of the homeless guy on the floor twitched, causing Walt to jump back.

"What did you see out there, Beaner?" Todd cornered me against one of the sinks and looked me in the eye.

"It could have been anything," I said.

"We don't have time for this." Todd paced the length of the bathroom, making Walt step out of his way. Todd was the least likely of all of us to overanalyze a problem.

He was in no danger of living out the rest of his life in a subway bathroom. I felt like I was depending on him to reach into me and unearth the inertia that had its grip on me and that was making it impossible for us to escape. My survival skills amounted to the fetal position, but Todd was the kind of guy who could take action, think up that lie that would fool the headmaster or stash the bong under his desk before the hall monitor walked in. In another setting, he had the charisma to be a detective, or maybe a stone-cold cowboy blasting his way out of an ambush. After his second circumnavigation of the bathroom, he banged his hand against an empty paper towel dispenser. He stepped over the rusty puddle next to the broken urinal and pulled off his backpack, dropping it and his Chinese takeout box on the ground next to one of the bathroom stalls.

"Walt's going to go take a look," he said, without bothering to address himself to Walt. "He's going to report back."

Walt's hands jumped up, and he touched his chest with his fingers, his eyebrows turning into sideways question marks. "Who, me?" he asked with his eyebrows, but Todd had his back turned so the question was mainly directed at me.

"But—" Walt started as Todd spun around and steered him toward the door.

"He doesn't know what you look like," Todd explained, pushing Walt out into the corridor. The door closed with a swallow, and the trickling water seemed to grow louder in the empty bathroom. Once we were alone, Todd looked at me, using one of the soaped-up mirrors to make eye contact. "What's with you, Beaner?" he asked, his pupils unwavering. He sounded as if he had been waiting all day to ask me that question, had arranged our solitude for just that purpose. I know that I had been moody, but I hadn't thought anyone had noticed. I occasionally have to check myself over to make sure that the world isn't seeing something I'm not. I noticed Todd's Snidley Whiplash mustache had vanished. Under the sharp light, I could just make out the shadow of where it had been.

"My eyes hurt," I said, making something up. The door swung open again and Walt came back, followed by a black guy in a wool hat.

"There's a problem," Walt said.

He moved over to let the black guy get to one of the working urinals. The guy seemed to take finding the three of us having a conversation in a bathroom in the basement of Grand Central pretty casually, though he gave a low whistle as he checked out my handshaker suit. At the urinal, his back to us, he peed a long stream that went on forever. I don't think any of us breathed until it trickled off. Most people have to take in their surroundings before they pee, and even then they take a minute or two to pee in front of an audience, if they can manage to do it at all. Each of us stared at the guy's back and waited and then looked down at our feet when he zipped up and swung around. He gave us a quick look, reached into his pocket, and dropped a couple of quarters into the homeless guy's Styrofoam cup. Then he stepped over one of the puddles and left the way he had come.

"What problem?" Todd asked when we were alone again, engulfed by the mournful drip, drip of the bathroom.

"I don't know what I'm looking for," Walt confessed.

Todd stared at me to let me know that the explanations were mine. "He's . . . " I started to describe and then thought about old Knees and the croquet games we used to play at the summerhouse in Maine. I remembered one in particular, a night when my mother was away for a meeting with her agent, when we had gone out on the lawn and he had bet me five bucks that I couldn't beat him. I had no athletic abilities, but I had won enough and under such unlikely circumstances that I had forgotten my suspicion that he was letting it happen. The evening air was full of mosquitoes, the bug zapper on the big back porch lighting one up every thirty seconds. Down by the water, we could hear but not see the lap, lap, lap of the waves on the rocks and the clang, clang, clang of the metal fasteners on Knees' sailboat banging against the mast. We played one game. I asked for a rematch, and we played six more games until I was in the hole thirty-five bucks. The humiliation of losing at sports has a tendency to piss me off, especially when a step is trying to take me down a peg, but Knees laughed when he told me to pay up. He swept off his phony captain's hat and made a bow. "To a worthy opponent," he said, which really got to me, hearing him say the word *worthy*.

Todd watched the convulsions taking place on my face as I struggled with my memories, and then he looked away. The dude hated weakness, hated anything that looked like it was going to bring him down, too, or remind him of his own frustrations, his mean brother, his deadbeat customers, but I couldn't hold myself in. Snot burned my nose and I sucked at it as I hoped and prayed he wouldn't disappear on me the way my mother had disappeared. I could tell he wanted to, could tell I had been striking out since Walt paid my train fare. One, two, three, back to the minors. If I could have, I would have hocked all the buttons on my suit just to pay him what I owed him. I would have let him keep the tie-dye he was already wearing and thrown in a couple of newer pairs of underwear. Though we had been randomly assigned to each other our first year, I needed him. In return, he needed me to crack a lot of stupid jokes when his friends were around. I made being fucked up look like fun, which was excellent advertising. I was no longer an accidental presence; I was an employee of the firm with certain corporate responsibilities, and I wanted to believe that everyone depended on me. Todd's expression suggested otherwise.

He resumed his pacing for one more cycle before he picked up his backpack and his Chinese takeout box and pushed them into my hands. I took the gifts without really understanding what he was giving me. I wondered what had made him pass these things over to me instead of taking them with him. It was a little like a movie scene in which three people trapped on an island decide that two of them are going to paddle for help, leaving the last of the Slim Jims with the guy left behind in case they don't return. After he had bestowed his worldly goods upon me, Todd grabbed Walt by the elbow and stepped backward toward the door. "We'll be right back," he said, and I believed him even though I had seen him teach other poor customers hard lessons. He pushed out into the tunnel. "Fifteen minutes," he said, holding up his hand with all five fingers and the flat of his palm facing me. The door swooshed shut again, and Walt and Todd were gone.

A train left the station and the walls rumbled. A piece of ceiling plaster dropped into one of the sinks, making me jump from my perch in the corner. The homeless guy grunted in his sleep and the Muzak kept playing. While I started counting seconds, the sinks dripped and the trains screeched in and rumbled out. The fifteen minutes stretched out to twenty. When Walt and Todd hadn't come back after twenty-five, in order to avoid the looks of guys coming in to use the urinals, I opened one of the stall doors and sat down on the toilet, drawing up my feet so no one would know I was there. Next to me, I noticed a hole in the partition a little larger than the size of a bullet. Above it, in red letters, somebody had written a poem: "Stick your dick in/and get a lick in." I bet I knew guys who would try it. Maybe Steve the hockey player would poke his thing in. I could see him making all kinds of sick comments about what happened next. I bet myself that Kenny J. would do it.

The hole wasn't big enough for a full-size johnson, though—it was barely big enough for a thumb—which meant my rumination on who would and wouldn't (Walt, no; Peas Passer, yes; Todd, maybe) was purely academic. Once I had all the particulars worked out and Todd still wasn't back, I opened his backpack. I found his Walkman, a couple of prerolled joints, three paper clips, duct tape, two Twinkies, the goddamned gun, and a roll of money bound up with a red rubber band. What I didn't find was show tickets or train schedules from Penn Station. Todd had those in his pocket and Todd and Walt were gone. Good luck to any dude who had to take my place. Kenny J. mouth breathed, wet the bed at night, and had a lousy collection of bootleg tapes. Walt wasn't cut out for the freak experience and represented a truly lousy profit potential, being a day student and all. I pictured Todd at forty, sitting around in some dark office, dwelling on his life, wondering whatever the hell had happened to me.

Probably that dude Skippy with the bitching stereo system would fill my shoes. What a joke. The first time Skippy came to our room to get high, he bogied a hit so badly that the bowl shot up out of the top of the bong and made a quarter-inch dent in the stucco wall, dope and bong water splashing all over everything. I cracked up while Skippy fiddled around trying to fix things by pretending he'd done it on purpose. I remember laughing until my sides hurt and that it felt good to be the one laughing instead of the one being laughed at. The poor guy was trying his level best to fit in, the very quality that would make him one more poor-sap friend in Todd's long line of poor-sap friends. The guy after me—that's who Skippy was destined to be.

There had been plenty of times when Skippy and Todd and I had hung out or taken rides to the grocery store together, normal things that didn't involve guns or terrorism. We'd go to the Westmarket or the Grand Union a couple of times a month and wheel our way through consumerland, buying stuff we needed, stealing stuff we didn't, small stuff like Budding beef and dog chew toys, stuff that could fit in the inside pocket of our handshaker suits. These trips made Skippy nervous, but for me they were joyous times.

I remember on one occasion we got trapped behind a teenage mommy in the fifty-seven-items-or-less line and her kid grabbed at the *People* magazine in the rack and dropped it to the floor. Todd picked it up, talking with the kid's mother while she negotiated her coupons, her money, and her groceries. I thought for sure Todd was going to snag one of the Twinkies from her Twinkie box, hit on her, maybe. When we got out to the car, he showed me the pink wallet he'd managed to pinch from her pocketbook. I'd never gotten to peek at anything belonging to a woman who was not my mother or grandmother before, and I was curious. Inside that pink purse was a picture of a guy in the marines who looked to be about twelve. There was another picture of a wrinkly baby wearing a white headband and pink dress. Way deep in, tucked in one of the secret money compartments, was a picture of the woman in a cheerleading outfit, looking not that much younger but a lot happier. We tossed the purse and her money on the sidewalk outside the store, but we kept the photographs, Todd snagging the one with her in the cheerleading outfit.

I thought about what Todd and Walt were doing out there in the station, getting caught or lost or tied up in traffic, in a kind of passive-aggressive attempt to be finished with a day that had never gotten around to going right for any of us. I imagined Walt tagging behind Todd and suddenly realizing that they weren't coming back for me. I wondered whether Walt would stick his neck out on my behalf or whether he, too, would try to stay on Todd's good side. I started to get angry, sitting there on the toilet seat, imagining them having a conversation about me, my mother, and my stepfather troubles, the way my pants never seemed to fit, the problems I had folding clothes. Unfortunately most prep schools instill an every-guy-for-himself ethic into their students. The whole ego-driven thing is designed to keep the upper-class economy going and help those of us with trust funds along to affording retirement. Up until then, I had thought it would be Walter who would be ditched, not me. That it was me meant Todd was moving on, washing his hands of the trouble I caused him and training a new bag man.

Croquet memories started flooding in again and

threatened to drown me in unwanted snot. I had always acted as if life were something to get your kicks from, but if you looked around, you'd notice that a lot of people weren't having a good time because they were either too broke or too sad or too sober to laugh it all off, and if they hadn't ever been abandoned in a bathroom under Grand Central by their best friends, then they'd probably experienced something similar. Happiness always seemed to exist in the past or in the future, not in the right now. People say "I remember" when they talk about a happy moment or "It's going to be great" when they're lying to themselves about the future. Either way, it's bullshit. Heaven is the biggest damn future-tense lie of them all. So, I thought, why not take the express train and arrive early at a heaven that isn't really heaven anyway? What would be the difference?

"Camera One." I covered one eye and looked toward the stall door.

"Camera Two." I moved my hand over and covered the second eye.

Not a whole lot of us actually take the suicide step, but what the hell keeps a person on this dirty, lousy planet anyway? I wasn't a morbid guy, and I didn't think about death often, but there was some part of me that felt removed from the rest. Thinking about my life while sitting on my toilet perch, I wanted to stick my head in and drown myself right then and there. I wanted to take Todd's gun from his backpack and play Russian roulette, find out if Todd had really put bullets in it. Never mind that I had already sworn off guns for the day and maybe for my whole life after what had happened in Walt's car. There was a guy at Stillwater, a junior when I was a freshman, who tried to off himself by taking a bunch of sleeping pills and curling up in one of the shower stalls. One of the hall monitors found him and called the proctor. I used to bump into him outside Dr. Keller's office. He always looked a mess coming out of his appointment, whereas I tried to make everyone believe I was comfortable with my neurosis, my mother being a member of the profession and all.

But I was sick of faking it and I wondered what joining Haley, my dead goldfish, in the sweet hereafter would be like. I wondered whether he would still have that mangled look, the look he had when we flushed him, or whether his unnecessary flesh would be made whole, whether he would be transformed into a spiritual cloud, warm in the way of a first springtime sunbeam. I pulled the .45 out of the backpack and looked at it, black in my hands. I opted for the sunbeam because if I pulled the trigger and blew my head off, I, too, would be looking at eternity in a hellish state, consigned to the part of the netherworld where the ugly dead had to hang out alone since the good-looking corpses would most likely want their own club. I imagined the homeless guy waking up from the sound of my shot, startled, the first to find me and the splatter of blood obscuring the writing on the walls of the stall. I imagined him putting his head to my heart—if he could even find my heart with all the bone and brains strewn about. I imagined him leaning in and listening for signs of life and not finding any, and I wondered what he would do then. Pick up his cup and leave, that's what he would probably do. That's what any sane guy would do.

I heard a bang outside the stall door, and my heart leaped because I thought I had gone ahead and done what I was only half telling myself to do, that for the second time that day I had been plugged with a bullet and the very thing I thought I held in my own hands—my dignity, my self-control, my life force—was at the mercy of someone else. I thought it might be Walt and Todd coming back, but then a pair of men's street shoes, the kind with tassels on top, passed in front of the stall door. I pulled my knees up closer to my chest and held my breath while the shoes padded their way around the homeless guy and across the tiles. The homeless guy rolled over and rattled his Styrofoam cup. "Spare some change?" he mumbled. It sounded more like "Sarah Fange," but the cup said what needed to be said.

The pair of shoes hesitated, I'm assuming because of how weird it was to see the guy come to life and ask for money. Then they padded into the stall next to mine. I listened to the usual noises, wondering if I should clear my throat so whoever belonged to them wouldn't get the wrong idea and think that he was alone. People do things when they think they're by themselves that they wouldn't necessarily do if they knew they had an audience. I pick my nose, for example. The person above the shoes whistled while he went, making it sound like the pee was arcing out the open door of an airplane to rain bombs on the world. The guy made small explosions as the stream hit the bowl. When he was finished, he banged out of the stall, stepped around the homeless guy, and dropped some change into the cup.

I peeked around the hinges to watch him wash his hands. He was the guy you'd catch peering down a waitress's shirtfront or buying macaroni and cheese in the grocery store for his bachelor dinner even though he was wearing an Italian suit and made a six-figure income. He was Captain Dog, of the Dog Eat Dog culture, a dude like Todd all grown up. It didn't look so damn hard to be him. I'd squashed Haley, eaten a hot dog instead of a Boca Burger at Sam's, and forced Peas Passer in front of my bullet. I had rained lovely little bombs with just as much ease as anyone else. But shit, man, I didn't dig whizzing on the world so shamelessly. I didn't like the pathetic dude I was either, a whiny bastard whose parents sent him off to a crappy half-assed school and whose friends had ditched him in a bathroom stall. I was alone, and only losers find themselves as alone as me.

Even Jerry had mysteriously deserted me, replaced by "Bridge over Troubled Water" playing a second time over the loudspeaker. God, that's a crappy song. I picked up the gun and waited for the dude with the tassels to finish pumping at the empty soap dispensers and admit he was going to have to take his dirty hands with him. My legs ached from sitting on the toilet seat and I shifted, nearly dropping Todd's Chinese takeout box onto the floor but stopping it with the hand that held the gun. Jerry was in the symbol on the top of the box. I saw his image as I reached, his little round glasses the small dot in the middle, his face half in and half out of the light, yin and yang, something to draw the pilgrims on down the line. I blinked and he was gone. I blinked again and he was back. And Jerry, I began to see, Jerry was the place where all the chaos collided and formed a whole. Jerry was a quark, man, an astrophysical beginning. Jerry was everywhere—he was even in the crappy Muzak, the bridge, maybe.

Another train rumbled through the station—the shuttle to Times Square. It was a quick scoot downtown from there to Penn Station, where the trains to Freedom waited. The jerk with the tassels left the sink and went out, leaving the water on and pissing me off for his insensitive indifference to precious resources. I took a breath and unbolted the door, shoved the gun in the backpack just to put it someplace. When I fiddled with the tap, the water kept running, flowing down and down. I twisted the handle and it still ran. Water is always running somewhere, and in my frustration to shut it off I recognized it was running in me. I could rap with the devil and blaze in my own glory. I stood there in the bathroom with my hand on the tap, feeling eternity flow through me.

Another dude came in, racing to the urinals before he was overwhelmed. The expression on his face was troubled and desperate, naked in the way no guy ever wanted to get caught naked in a public bathroom. In order to give him some privacy, I hunted through my pockets for some change, found my fuzzy nickel, and dropped it in the homeless guy's Styrofoam cup. Unsure that that would be enough, I took off my peacoat and dropped that next to him, too. The homeless guy looked peaceful despite the discombobulation of his body and his shirt, which twisted around so far that some of the buttons faced the ceiling while the rest of him faced the floor. Even in his comatose state, he had made a profit—and also gained a peacoat in the last hour, and there was still hope for more before the day ended.

My next few steps were difficult, existentially, but also because the floor was slippery. I slung Todd's backpack over my shoulder and walked into the tunnel, where not many people were milling around—not many for Grand Central anyway, just the guys who swept and the guys who are always there: the pickpockets, dope dealers and scam artists, the cops who were trying to bust them, and, finally, the guys who played instruments looking for quarters. I accepted that I had a destination, music I wanted to hear, a tape I wanted to record. I was in that line of dancing bears again and the gravity of joy was pulling me forward.

No question about it, Grand Central was Dante-inspired, or a regular Talmudic universe with the saddest and lowest levels of humanity on the bottom and the more heavenly levels toward the top. I climbed stairs and wound through corridors until I rose to the main terminal, suddenly amazed at what a fantastically beautiful place it was, with crystal chandeliers and marble floors, angels painted on the ceiling, all this under only a slight layer of grime and soot, like it was true beauty waiting to be rediscovered. My mood began to lift, maybe even soar too high. I spun around under the domed ceiling of the terminal, drawing the momentary attention of people passing by. I would have tossed my hat in the air if I'd had a hat, that's how much I felt like I had just become the starring character in my own situation comedy.

On my second turn, I caught sight of a guy selling roses. Saint Stephen, I thought. "Saint Stephen with a rose," I sang, and got the scorn I so richly deserved. Before I'd wandered into the bathroom, a zillion of my stepfathers had seemingly lingered under every cigarette sign, but now that I had come out, the faces were sharper, distinct, the Tin Man, the Cowardly Lion, and Auntie Em, and though I had ridden a whirlwind to wake to them, they were here and I could see them. I looked up at the slats on the boards, and then I pushed my way out the door onto Forty-second Street. I ran out onto the sidewalk, past the porter with the silver whistle, and into the smog from the cued line of cabs. I jumped into the last cab in the row and damn if the driver wasn't Pigpen McKernan, Jerry's dead keyboardist. Not dead. Not forgotten. Just receding into life so far down nobody would ever look.

"Take me to Freedom," I said.

He glanced up from a clipboard on which he was writing himself notes. I whipped out the one hundred fifty or so dollars Todd had left behind when he had pushed his backpack into my arms and told me to wait.

"Take me to the show," I said.

And, hot damn, he did.

DIRE WOLF

I F YOU LOOK at Jerry's life as a continuum, then you'll find Ron "Pigpen" McKernan on the darkest edge, along with a few of his Hells Angels buddies and some of the Merry Pranksters who had a gritty side as well. Pigpen supposedly died a well-deserved death due to overconsumption, and it was only by hearing my stepfather Knees explain the history of the sixties that I understood how deep Jerry's roots went. Of course, I had known that freaks had worshipped Jerry for some time, but I did not know the forms their devotion had taken—the hazy days of Woodstock, the tragedy of Altamont. My stepfather Knees had been in San Francisco during 1968, not so much protesting the Vietnam War as attending a boat show, and he had been "this close" to Jerry in an airport once but had not reached out and touched him.

I asked my stepfather if he knew anyone who had been invited to the "electric Kool-Aid" acid tests, but he said no, he was in law school on the East Coast at the time. He said that he had seen LSD mess up a lot of young lives. I clued in finally that his version of the sixties was meant to be a cautionary tale, but I enjoyed the details and how much my stepfather seemed to be extending in my direction, so I asked him more questions.

"Was my mother there?" I asked.

We both knew that my mother never missed a party, but Knees shook his head, saying he didn't think so, and then he did the math for me, pointing out that she would have been only twelve years old at the time. We were having the conversation over one of our croquet games, of course, where we had all our happiest chats, and I asked him if he missed living in the Dawn of Aquarius. He hesitated before answering and ran his hands down to his knees as he knelt to line up a shot. He said that they were sincere times. Then he took his mallet and knocked his ball into mine. This made him chuckle, and he put his foot on my ball and swung his mallet so hard that the ricochet sent me (not me literally but me symbolically—

my little orange ball) into one of the tidal pools down by the beach. That was the end of the orange ball, but we never missed it, seeing as we had others and it was only Knees and I who had ever used the set.

Meanwhile Pigpen McKernan, not dead but driving the evening shift for a New York City cab company, looked up at me in his rearview mirror.

"Freedom, Long Island?" he asked, double-checking.

All I could see of him was the back of his head behind the scratched bulletproof plastic partition and his forehead framed by the rectangle of the rearview mirror. I nodded while he checked me out, his eyes swimming up into the glass and floating there for a minute. He looked at my Stillwater uniform, the gold buttons on my blazer, and the wad of green I had pulled out of the pack in an attempt to solidify my credibility. I heard a low whistle, as if he was deciding that I was one of those stories he was going to have to tell back at the garage. He considered what he saw for a second: the silver spoon sticking out of my mouth, the six digits in my trust fund, and what looked like enough cash to take me to Topeka, Kansas—but what was really only a couple of tens wrapped around 130 ones. Pigpen pulled up the front of his leather pancake hat and ran a hand over his almost-hidden bald spot. He had long, scraggly hair drooping into a ponytail and a wide neck with three horizontal folds running from one side of his nape to the other. While I held my breath and hoped, he unhooked his radio from the clamp underneath the dashboard and spoke into it.

"Got a fare out to Long Island," he said, his voice rumbling up from deep down in his throat, sounding like he had just finished gargling the East River. After a while, the radio crackled back acknowledgment: "Cab one-four-two, roger that."

The money I offered Pigpen wasn't mine—it was Todd's—but I decided as I held it out that Todd wouldn't mind me borrowing some of it, or all of it, especially since he probably had more cash in his pocket and this was just his seed money for future transactions. I promised myself he would get it all back with interest when my next allowance check arrived or when I made him a copy of the three-star tape I would record once I got to Freedom. Even if I never saw Todd again, I figured he could hold the stuff in our room as collateral. I had done a good job tie-dyeing the underwear on the floor, and I bet some of the newer pairs were marketable.

The alternative to taking my chance with Pigpen was lugging the pack back into Grand Central and hopping the subway to Penn Station for a Long Island train. I would have to descend into the tunnel again, which I didn't want to do now that I had surfaced. I also had my reasons for not wanting to be late, getting a ticket being one of them, but also being able to push my way in close to the soundboard and giving myself time to dose a little acid. I could have hitched a ride, stuck my thumb out and hoped for the best, but the best hardly ever happened in Manhattan (more like the worst: muggings, stabbings, or just general harassment by the locals). I was trapped by circumstances, it seemed to me, and I was going to have to make do with what I had. If the dollars didn't exactly square up at the end of the night, then it would be just one more psychic debt I owed the world.

"Nice evening," I said to Pigpen, but it wasn't nice. The mist had lifted, but icy rain dripped down in front of the station and formed deep puddles on the sidewalk.

Pigpen, or Zebulon Nash, as the identification card hanging from the dashboard had labeled him, didn't respond. He seemed to have something weightier on his mind than the quality of the weather. He punched the top of the meter and started the counter rolling, expressing his disgust for the cold coffee he had just bought at the deli and the number of pedestrians streaming through the crosswalk. He missed getting the mouthpiece of the radio back into its holder and heaved it onto the floor instead, meanwhile punching more numbers into the meter. The coiled cord that attached to the mouthpiece thumped back up underneath the dashboard, finally settling on a lump between the seats. Even when they do speak English, cabbies in New York are distant and preoccupied and, as a rule, hostile to the poor fools they've taken in out of the rain. While I stuffed the money back into the pack, Zebulon shifted the cab into drive and steered a course through the traffic on Forty-second Street, the icy rain splattering onto the windshield and sticking to the wipers. He clearly liked driving better than waiting for a fare, liked getting out from under the claustrophobic overhang of Grand Central into the murk of the street. He wound the engine out, making the gears in the automatic transmission strain and the tires skid. We banked a corner, and I slid sideways on the seat into one of the inside door handles, catching it on my elbow. Like most

New York City cabs, the seats were worn slick.

"Ouch," I complained.

"Hang on, kid." Pigpen banked again onto Madison Avenue, and I went sliding the other way.

If being on the road made Pigpen feel better, it made me feel good again, too, even though I was pummeled every time we took a corner. I wondered if my driver really was Pigpen, and I gave some thought to asking him for an autograph. My asking would probably have pissed him off, since just about everything seemed to piss him off: the white sedan in front of us, the construction that closed down one lane and kept him from cutting a guy off. I'm not usually the starstruck type. Some of my favorite television shows starred people my mother entertained at cocktail parties or who were the parents and friends of other sad summer campers at Lake Misapasawkie. I remember seeing the Six Million Dollar Man having a toke on the porch of our summerhouse and wondering whether the six-million-dollar asshole thought that the taxpayers had another six million to redo his lungs and heart, too. I liked dope, but I wasn't the one fighting off fem-bots and saving the world. I had no illusions about the nature of celebrities, just the occasional blurred vision that cleared when I blinked. Still, an autograph from Jerry's dead keyboardist would have been something.

I watched the wet brownstones and shops pass by the cab, apartment windows with spider plants hanging from the sills, people in raincoats, open umbrellas, and dogs straining against their leashes. So much of the world passed by that I got to feeling hopeful. I reminded myself that I had arrived at more than one show without a ticket in my pocket or having smoked all the weed I'd packed for the trip. Somehow or another, Jerry always provided. A freak would pass me a pipe when I started to jones, or the show would turn into general admission because of the size of the crowd. Believing in Jerry was the best kind of credit I could get. It was like carrying my stepfather's gold card. I decided I was doing the driver a favor, putting our fate into Jerry's hands. The cab lurched around another corner, and I wondered whether old Pigpen had ever damaged anybody besides himself with his recklessness, had ever pitched anybody out of a not-quite-locked back door, just sent them skittering out into the street or up onto the curb like a morning newspaper. Up in the front, he rubbed his bloodshot eyes with a meaty knuckle instead of watching the red light gleaming ahead of us.

In my philosophical frame of mind, I got to thinking that the road outside was like the hyphens in my name, Scotty Emerson-Fitzgerald-Douglas, propelling itself endlessly outward with each new person my mother married. The road made all of the thoughts I'd had about croquet while trapped at Grand Central Terminal seem sentimental. I was no longer Mr. Loveletter, Little Freak, Beaner, Scotty Douglas, or Little Loveletter. I was no longer Prince of Croquet, Knight of the Wickets. I was the road at last.

I thought of Knees in some midtown bachelor apartment, the one he had undoubtedly rented when he moved his things out of the Connecticut house. He would just be coming home, taking off his raincoat and getting himself ready to slice up some shiitake mushrooms for stir-fry. He'd have been tied up in weekend meetings until six or six-thirty, nowhere near Grand Central as I had feared—and if there was a message on the machine from my mother telling him that I had run away from school, he wouldn't have the faintest idea of where to look for me. He wouldn't want to know. I was water under the bridge. Who could blame him for thinking otherwise?

The meter fixed to Zebulon's dashboard read $22,

and the numbers kept rolling. At first I paid no attention. I was now free to blow off school and join a commune if I wanted or to live at one of those hippie resorts with a big repainted bus that drove people to the shows every summer. I was free to stretch out on a piece of cardboard in a train bathroom if I felt like it. Now that I was the master of my own destiny, fatherless and personal finances–less, I was free to do most anything I wanted. The future was a clean piece of paper, my hopes and dreams a big box of Crayola crayons. I was past the artificial obligations of impending tolls and psychic debts. Money is the worst kind of evil there is, especially when you have too much of it, as I sometimes did, or not enough of it, as could also happen. I knew plenty of guys whose only friends were people who hung out with them in order to improve their monetary situation. I felt sorry for people with a lot of income, since once you got the hang of it, blowing a generous amount of cash was easier than blowing your nose. You just needed to develop some discipline and familiarity with the Sharper Image catalog to do it.

We crossed the 59th St. Bridge and passed empty warehouses and small bent trees. Zebulon turned on the radio, cranking the volume. A Christmas pipe organ selection boomed live over the airwaves from St. John the Divine. The music was like an angry announcement that the holidays were upon us. Peace on Earth, goodwill toward men, and all that aggressive premerchandising foulness. Outside the cab, the bustle of Queens flitted by like a dream, the sky a smog-shrouded memory and the rain heavy and black on the streets. I took another look at Zebulon's identification picture. He was a beady-eyed monster and I wondered whether he'd ever killed a man. Pigpen was by far the meanest member of the Grateful Dead, and I sometimes wondered whether the rest of the band didn't just buy the guy out, he was such a mismatch, such a long way from anybody's idea of sunshine daydreams.

While I watched Zebulon from the backseat, he glanced up every so often and snuck a peek at me in the rearview mirror. The inside of the passenger area was littered with the debris of his former customers—the dirt from their shoes, the smell of sweat and alcohol from the parties they had just left, and even the lingering smell of cigarette smoke (even though there was a big red NO SMOKING sign bolted to the seat in front of me and not an ashtray in sight). I wondered whether Zebulon had ever thought about giving up the driving business and hitting the highway for California, having a road adventure. We'd be Neal and Jack, or Huck and Jim, the Road Runner and old Wile E.

"What's new?" I asked him.

It wasn't much of a question, but it broke some of the chilliness that had lasted through the first fifteen minutes of the ride, the time we had spent sizing each other up and taking each other's psychic measure.

He shrugged.

I wondered whether Zebulon had been trying to figure out what my life was like, mistaking my enthusiasm about being on my own for the fantasizing of a poor little rich kid. For about the hundredth time that day, I wanted to shout that rich people have feelings and some of us don't feel so entitled to our stuff; more like the opposite, more like we'd been cursed by what we have been given, and that somehow, someway, we were going to have to give it all back. The meter glowed from the dashboard, an evil red eye, the numbers doubling and tripling themselves at an unnatural rate of speed. We had barely made it out of Manhattan. Zebulon followed my glance and something twitched in his face, a stifled laugh or a shudder, someone walking over his grave, maybe—hard to say what—and then he hit something on the meter so that the numbers started rolling a little faster even than before.

"Holiday rate," he said. "Almost forgot." Then he readjusted his mirror to look out past me into the traffic behind us.

I began to think about how I might ditch Zebulon. Back at Stillwater, Todd and I occasionally asked a driver to drop us off at a mall or a supermarket or someplace with a lot of people, and while he or she was writing down the fare on a clipboard, we'd lose ourselves in the melee faster than you could say "Jumping Jack Flash," going two directions at once so as to force the driver to make a choice about which one of the two of us to nab first. Cabbies in the town of Stillwater were slow, overweight, and out of shape, and the wheezy pursuit that followed was just a formality, unpaid cab fare a common enough occurrence that the company could call up the school and complain to get the money back. This made hell for us with the proctors and the headmaster, but it was worth it if it meant restocking the mini-fridge. There were differences between a Stillwater cabbie and Zebulon worth mulling over—I bet he had fifty-six priors. I was also going to owe him a lot more than twelve bucks at the end of the night.

"What's the seven-ninety for?" I asked, pointing to a group of numbers at the top of the meter that he had punched in after putting in the "holiday rate." Zebulon adjusted the mirror to look back at me again, his eyes a pair of blue fish swimming in a polluted ocean of yellow-and-red-streaked iris.

"Per person customer charge," he said.

"What?" I asked, incredulous.

"One fare—that's you," he said. He had the look my math teacher got when the answer to the equation was obvious to everyone but me.

He must have thought I was a patsy, born yesterday. I couldn't believe his nerve, trying to rip me off. We passed a tour bus at an accelerated rate of speed, and before I could get to the door handle to hang on, we were on the exit to the LIE, the side of the road a littered mess of beer cans and donut boxes, other traffic whipping past us despite our own speed. It was starting to get deeply dark, which it did now as early as five o'clock in the afternoon, and the rat color of the sky permeated the landscape. One of the other things I had forgotten to bring with me on my trip to Freedom, in addition to tickets, money, food, and the right kind of clothing, was a watch to tell me what time it was. I depended on Todd for that, too: the record of my daily routine. Stillwater Academy, with its military arrangement of my life, had conditioned me to mishandle any free or unplanned time. I was at a complete loss without the crutch of ringing bells and mandatory events.

"How much longer?" I asked. I thought it might be time to jump ship.

"You in a hurry?" Zebulon seemed surprised. "You want me to drop you off right here?" He swerved experimentally toward a traffic island surrounded by asphalt and trash. He pumped the brakes of the cab.

"No, no." I broke my forward momentum on the seat in front of me.

"You got a date with destiny?" he asked, pumping the brakes again, really slowing down this time. "A little snot-nosed Tiny Tim Cratchit like yourself?" He indicated my blue blazer and the tie, which I was still wearing for some damn reason. I thought about telling him that Tiny Tim Cratchit hopped around on a crutch and had no figgy pudding for Christmas, but he didn't look like he wanted his literary allusions corrected. I should have taken my tie off on the train, but the need to stay square for the Barbara Bush–alikes had made me forget. Instead of taking it off now, I squirmed in my seat as Zebulon bumped the cab up onto the shoulder.

"Why are you stopping?" I asked him, my voice slightly hysterical.

The traffic island looked like a good place to dump a corpse and I wondered how many bodies Zebulon had piled up here and how long it was going to take the police to catch up with him once he had done me in. He looked like the type who would use piano wire, but maybe he had an ice pick lying around. I was reaching for the door handle when Zebulon grabbed his empty Styrofoam coffee cup and crumpled it with his fist. He had something tattooed on his knuckle and a big skull ring on his left hand. I imagined the headline the next morning: "Boy Found Beaten by Skeleton—Foul Play Suspected." Into the eye sockets of the skull were set red rubies that glowed in the gloom.

"Need to take a piss," Zebulon said. He opened the door and tossed the cup into the littered night. When the door swung open, the inside of the cab flooded with light, blinding me temporarily and then making me see blue spots after it swung shut again. I heard Zebulon crunching through the sleet into the shadow of an exit sign and I heard the sound of his relieving himself against the back left tire.

"Yeah," I said to no one in particular.

I had begun to sweat, and the duct tape holding the sheet of acid against my chest itched. I leaned forward and looked up through the bulletproof glass to see whether the keys were still in the ignition. They were. The turn signal was still on, still click, click, clicking, making music along with the organ, the pattering rain, and the sweeping windshield wipers. I slid back into my seat, wondering what I was going to do, remembering the .45 in Todd's backpack and wishing that I knew how to use it. I pulled my blue oxford shirt out of my pants and started to scratch. While I was scratching, Zebulon finished his business and opened the driver's-side door, flooding the interior of the cab with light again. I winced, and he looked back at me. I wasn't sure, but I thought he might have glimpsed the acid duct-taped to my chest. In any case, he smiled.

"Well well well," he said, making the same low whistle

he had made when I had gotten into the cab.

I didn't know what the hell he was going on about. What had I done? I had gotten into his cab, and I had asked him for a ride. He was a cabbie, for Christ's sake. I wanted to tell him to turn around and mind his own business, but before I had the chance, he turned around anyway and faced forward in his seat. The cab lurched as he dropped it into gear, and the meter, which he left running when he stepped out of the cab, was now reading more than forty dollars.

Zebulon accelerated, and I put my head on the back of the seat in front of me and broke eye contact with him in the rearview mirror. He swerved sideways into traffic to get around a slow truck and then headed out into the inescapable yellow dimness of the expressway ahead of us. The radio signal from the service at St. John's went out, and suddenly I could hear the sound of my own heart beating and a new river of thoughts coursing inside my head.

I hadn't heard the pipe organ until I stopped hearing it, and its absence was a painful, aching loss. I started to have my doubts about putting my life in the hands of a psychopath. Maybe because of the stress I had been under all day, or maybe because I was just tired, I started to freak out, and by "freak out," I mean hyperventilate. Zebulon looked over his shoulder through the bullet-proof glass and then turned his attention back to the road. I wasn't really doing or saying anything to get his attention, just breathing funny. When I was a little kid, I used to have attacks all the time, times where I would cry until I couldn't breathe. Now, if I was having a bad day, I just smoked a doobie or drank a beer, and everything settled down eventually. I tried to sit back, enjoy the scenery, and let myself go for a ride, but it wasn't coming naturally.

A good sense of proportion didn't run in my family. My mother and I were always overreacting. A couple of months before my mother's decision to do the *Playboy* spread, her Mercedes convertible wound up in the bottom of the pool, perhaps the first sign that she and Knees were splitting apart. She had driven it there herself, had steered it straight through the garage and over the patio. She got a big kick out of her exploits, whereas when I overreacted, I was riddled with shame for months afterward. An hour after the Mercedes incident, my mother and Knees were already cuddled on the couch, drying off, drinking Pernod, and joking about how much they were going to have to tip the pool man at the end of the week. The whole incident got recorded in our family history as the second-to-worst thing any one of us had ever done to a car and illustrated how a big thing could be a little thing if you gave yourself time to laugh it off.

"Look, kid . . . " Zebulon pulled a cigarette from his pocket, lit it one-handed, and tossed the match out the window.

When I was ten I had a nanny who lit cigarettes like Zebulon while whipping me up dinner. I was pretty indoctrinated then and I showed her a picture I had gotten in health class of a guy with a tube down his throat. She didn't react, but the next day, my mother called me down to the living room. She asked me to sit in a chair made from steel and leather, more of an art object than a landing pad. I did as she said, sliding back and back into the chair. My mother said, "Honey, please don't scare the help," but I didn't listen. I started collecting those pamphlets you can pick up at the doctor's office, and I snuck down to the wing of the house the nanny was in and slipped them under the door to her apartment, not so much saving her life as hoping to get another chance to see her look as she stared death in the face. It was a cheap way to get my kicks, but I was young and she was like having a rock or a stone for company, and that's how I rationalized it. I noticed that the silence of the radio had made Zebulon quiet and contemplative, too. Perhaps he was remembering his own nannies.

"Look, if I snapped at you . . . " Zebulon lifted his cap again, scratched the top of his head, and eased the tension out of his neck. "Look, man, we've all got our problems," he said finally.

He turned to glance over his shoulder, and I could see his handlebar mustache more clearly, along with a lot of other miscellaneous hair that hadn't been on his face when he had had the identification picture taken and that I could only get a hint of when he was turned the other way. His eyes, unframed by the rearview mirror, were ringed by a set of dark circles. As if to explain his sudden change in personality, he pulled a wallet-sized studio photograph from a clip on the sun visor and handed it back through the money slot.

"I got a daughter, and the ex-girlfriend won't let me see her for Christmas," he told me. He didn't wait to see how I was going to respond; he kept right on going as if

I weren't there. "'Christmas don't count as a weekend,'" he said, imitating his girlfriend's voice and pursing his lips. "Like I was going to have much work on Christmas Day," he said. "I can put the kid in the cab with me, I tell her, and she starts screaming child abuse."

I handed Zebulon back his picture. I asked him if his kid lived in Connecticut, but he said "Fuck, no" like he had never heard a question so mindless.

"Child abuse," he repeated. I told him I knew all about it.

Zebulon became quiet again, moody. He disappeared inside of himself like a rock dropped into a pool. Outside the tunnel, melted snow dotted the edges of the road and mixed in with the silver wedges of trash littering the ground. In the city, there had been only rain and puddles, a cleansing wetness, but here we were face-to-face with something like the elements. A Volkswagen bus splattered with brightly colored paint and bumper stickers that read "Listen to the Fat Man" and "Have a Merry Jerry" passed us. I got excited thinking about Freedom ahead of me, and I yelled over the pipe organ music.

"Did you see that?"

I pointed out the Volkswagen bus, now ahead of us

in traffic, weaving a little, and full to the brim with celebrants in the magical mystery cult of Jerry. The meter on the dashboard rolled up to fifty dollars, and Zebulon pulled another cigarette from the pocket of his vest, lighting it one-handed, then detaching the match from the book and tossing it out the window. Lighting cigarettes one-handed is a risky endeavor, and I kept waiting for him to set the cab on fire. Still, it was a pretty neat trick—one, I bet, he'd practiced in his jail cell. He could easily have been an old friend of Jerry's, one of his Hells Angels compadres from way back when. Jerry's old friends mostly had faded to gray and, like Jerry, had softened with age. Sometime in the late seventies, Jerry became the jolly fat guy on the cover of *Rolling Stone* that everybody identified with. He had that beatific voice, that ability to lilt just above the sound of his acoustic, which made people think of angels and made the tracks he sang memorable. It was that voice that made it possible for people like me to forgive him for starting a clothing line that included ties that even the worst and most avaricious of my stepfathers might have been caught wearing.

I realized I was lucky to have come across Zebulon's cab at Grand Central Terminal. I could have hopped into any cab, but I had picked his, the last in the line, the saddest, the one with paint chipping off the sides, a big dent in the front fender. The others under the lights on the street seemed too cheerfully yellow, too scrubbed, too much like the shiny faces of the teenagers who worked at the Grand Union. If Todd and Walt had still been with me, it would have been Todd who would have chosen the cab, using a set of criteria that I had begun trusting less and less since parting company with him. I wondered for the hundredth time that night where Todd and Walt were and decided that they had gone on, making their Penn Station connection as planned and getting into Freedom with an hour to spare. I imagined Todd hovering around the doors to the coliseum, getting slightly testy about having left me with his money and the acid and making poor Walt bum dope off the freaks in line next to him.

I hoped that Walt had some money with him, because without the cash in the backpack, Todd would not have enough for two train fares home. Walt would have to hitch, which usually worked out better leaving a show than arriving at one since people trying to get to the show are like every idiot on a schedule, impatient and crabby, but people leaving are blissed out and would hand you their last nickel. If he was going to handle the trip back to Connecticut, Walt would also have to get wasted. The rides I'd hitched back to Stillwater from a show had been rife with experimental drugging-and-driving practices. I'd ridden with drivers who wanted to know what happened when you used the other side of the dividing line or went down a road whose sign said DO NOT ENTER. I'd lived to talk about it, and since I was fucked up, too, I didn't mind too much—though Walt, because he was straighter, might. There had been this one ride we'd gotten from a freak lady who never once stepped on the accelerator pedal or moved off the shoulder. We squeaked it back about ten minutes before class. She let us roll a million joints from her stash in her backseat.

"Shit," Zebulon said through cigarette-clenching lips, punching the brakes to avoid rear-ending the Volkswagen. I wasn't exactly sure how to take the comment. Was the Volkswagen bus with the Jerry stickers shit or was I shit? Was he afraid of being recognized as the undead Pigpen by the bus's slew of wasted-looking passengers?

"How old are you, kid?" he asked.

"Twenty-two," I answered.

Zebulon glanced up at his rearview mirror and

wheezed. In his identification picture, he was wearing the same black leather vest and pancake hat that he currently had on, and his eyes crossed a little. In the picture, I could see the tattoo on his forearm: the head of an eagle with a snake in its mouth. Zebulon fiddled with a knob on the dashboard and blasted the heat. At the same time, he rolled down the window and put another cigarette between his lips. Peanut shells fluttered up from the floor around my feet, and I was simultaneously cold at the top of my head and scalp and sweating in my shoes, even though I was still not wearing socks.

I decided that Zebulon wasn't as scary as he looked. Hell, for all I knew, he could have been some kind of a Buddha, though I thought better of asking him to divulge his wisdom at that particular moment. After one more cigarette, Zebulon coughed and threw the empty pack out the window. I looked out the back of the cab and watched the cellophane glittering in the dark as the box first fluttered and then landed by the side of the highway. Behind us, the traffic folded into itself like the teeth on a zipper as the lanes narrowed down in a construction area. In some places, the highway had risen above the roads that ran parallel.

The pipe organ was behind us now, and after wrestling with some static, Zebulon snapped the radio off. In the silence, he began whistling something that might have been Jerry-inspired. The meter ticked up to one hundred ten dollars. I thought about asking Zebulon to pull into a rest stop. A sign for one had appeared outside the cab, but I was too late, and I saw the yellow service station lights disappear into the gloom. The meter ticked up to one hundred twenty-three dollars just past the exit for the Meadowbrook State Parkway.

"How old is your daughter?" I asked.

"I don't know." He seemed surprised by the question. He took another picture down from his visor and slipped it back through the slot to me. There she was, dressed in a yellow playsuit with a baseball patch on the front and hair as red as a pencil eraser. Two redheaded kids in one day, what were the odds? I thought of Kenny J.'s red ball popping in and out of his pocket. I thought of the orange croquet ball still sitting in the tidal pool by the house in Maine. I must have looked at the picture for a while because when I glanced up, Zebulon was staring at me.

"What are you looking at?" Zebulon asked.

"Nothing," I lied.

"Better not be," he said. "She's too young."

I passed the picture back through the money slot. Zebulon retrieved it and tossed it up onto the dash with a pile of other pictures and gas receipts. Something had shifted in his mood again, like he wanted to get his boss outside and go a few rounds with him or like he had a bone to pick with me. He didn't say anything for a while, and then he turned to talk over his shoulder. "You know what I hate?" he asked. One tip of his handlebar mustache brushed his leather vest as he turned to fix me with the corner of his eye.

"What?" I asked, afraid of every possible answer.

"I hate . . . " He looked forward and back into his mirror at me and then up in front of him to merge back into the slow lane. I felt my breathing stiffen in my chest again.

"I hate having to pee twice on a limited-access highway," Zebulon said, and he laughed his snaky laugh.

He pulled off onto the side of the road. Although I'm not sure he meant to, he left the meter running again. I stayed inside, listening once more to his urine streaming and then trickling and the windshield wipers scraping away the sleet. After a few minutes, he got into the cab and we moved into the night. When we finally got to Freedom, I gave up my thoughts of ditching him or plugging him with Todd's .45. My guess was that Zebulon was equally armed and that I never would have stood up to him in a shootout. Besides, I would have regretted killing him. He was an honest old fool, full of meanness rather than bullshit friendliness. I said nothing when he pulled into the parking garage, adding another six dollars to my total, and when he stopped, I forked over the dollars I did have, hoping he wouldn't want me around while he counted them. I even told him to keep the change as I picked up Todd's pack and started walking away, convinced that we were square.

"Hold it, kid," he said after I had gotten three feet. I felt my nape itch from the intentness of his gaze.

That's when he told me that I had two choices, and I chose the not-dying choice. I rustled through the pack and pulled out Todd's Chinese takeout carton, which Zebulon took and opened. There were some Rice Krispies inside, from a box that we had left sitting around our room for more than a month for want of some milk—and a dead toad. The Rice Krispies made me remember that Todd had been messed up when we had left Stillwater, and the toad made me think he had been trying to replace Haley, which kind of touched me. The second thing I pulled out was a box of tapes. Todd had packed a couple of ripping two-stars and one really bad one-star with Bobby singing "Eternity" for just about an eternity. Zebulon looked at the tapes, spat, and tossed them on the pavement. He wiggled his fingers for me to keep going. I pulled out the Walkman and two joints. He took the weed and the Walkman and slung them into the front of the cab. The last thing in the pack except for my wet socks was the .45 Peacemaker, which I was afraid as hell to show him because I knew he'd want it and because I knew that Todd would kill me if I lost it—or Zeb might plug me just for practice. I pulled my wet, reeking socks out of the bag and was handing them over when Zebulon stopped me.

"Ooh. Never mind," he said, waving them away with one hand and holding his nose with the other.

When he had regained his composure, he pointed at me and said, "Lose the clothes," his voice far dryer than it had been, absolutely devoid of smoker's phlegm. This obviously was his business voice. I'd noticed that people changed their voices to do business, and Zebulon was no exception.

I wasn't going to argue with him. I dropped the bag and started wrestling with my tie. I had my usual trouble with the buttons of my oxford shirt, but Zebulon seemed patient. He took the jacket of my handshaker suit, checked the pockets, and tossed it on the wet hood of the cab. He did the same with the shirt. A group of freaks passed us—two long-haired crunchy types and a girl in Birkenstocks. They walked a little faster, their heads down, even though I'm guessing they had seen stranger things on their way to a show than a guy standing in a pair of tie-dyed tighty-whities and a second scary guy asking him to strip.

"The jacket's worth one hundred ninety-three bucks," I told Zebulon, hoping he would take it and be done with me. "The buttons are real gold," I told him, even though I was pretty sure they weren't. My mother had been forced to buy it and three others like it when I'd been accepted at Stillwater. The khakis and button-down oxford shirt had some value, too, but I wasn't sure for what, maybe wiping up oil spills. I knew what Zeb wanted, though, what he had been after the whole time. His eyes were glowing like the rubies in his skull ring.

"What's this worth?" Zebulon asked, indicating the acid taped to my chest.

We stood staring at each other, his eyes going hard while I held my hands protectively against the sheet.

"I need it," I said. "You can't have it."

Zebulon folded his arms. I was a little surprised that I was able to drive any kind of bargain with him, but we came to some terms. He ripped the tape off my chest quickly to cause me as little pain as possible. I wasn't endowed with chest hair, but if I'd had any, it wouldn't have stood a chance against Zebulon's vigor. We set up a small business, selling hits to freaks on the top story of the parking garage. Zebulon made me put back on the suit, tie and all, saying that I needed to dress for success. Together, as business partners, we made about one hundred ninety-eight dollars, most of it going to him to pay for the fare and what he called a good tip. I used what I had made to buy back the Walkman and a few hits to dose with at the show. I asked him to join me inside, but he wheezed something between a laugh and a snort. Maybe he didn't want to blow his cabbie cover. I'd have to say, after watching him in action, that old Zebulon was a natural, better even than Todd at collecting his due.

About a half sheet into our business, a skinny, messed-up freak edged to the side of the cab and pulled a few crumpled dollar bills out of his pocket. Zeb laughed at him, too, in a hissing-snake kind of way.

"Seven bucks," he said, overcharging the guy by about forty percent. While the guy looked at him, dumbfounded, Zeb nudged me with his elbow.

"Holiday rate," he said.

FIRE ON THE MOUNTAIN

I GOT MY FIRST glimpse of the Freedom crowd from the top of the parking garage, just after I said good-bye to Zebulon. The swirl of tie-dye and Guatemalan sweaters filled up the entire north side courtyard and could have been a family reunion, the progeny of a couple of really prolific hippies. Everybody looked alike, dressed in Birkenstocks and wool socks, Indian print skirts, and love beads. Everyone seemed to share the same blissed-out expression—plate-sized pupils and wide, crazy grins—and I suppose Zeb and I were partially to thank. It was cold and drizzly out, thirty-two degrees, but you wouldn't have known it. Frisbees zipped through the air and landed in the puddles on the pavement. Soggy Hacky Sacks biffed back and forth inside circles of long-haired dope smokers. The high-summer atmosphere and haze of sunshine daydreams were in complete opposition to the murk of a November day in the Northeast, proving my longtime belief that Dead Heads made up the one social unit on the planet that didn't depend on reality to make itself happy.

In order to leave, Zebulon had had to negotiate arriving knots of showgoers getting out of their cars, driving up the down ramps, and skateboarding from level to level, and I could hear the horn cursing as he descended. Finally the yellow rectangle of his cab pushed its way through the throng below me into the beautiful beckoning swirl of humanity. I decided that my best chance for finding Walt and Todd or someone to sell me a ticket at a much-discounted price was in entering the vortex. The courtyard seemed to be where most of the buying and selling was going on, where the small strands of people had formed bigger tangles, looking from my vantage point like the gathering storms of a weather front seen from a satellite.

I have to say, I was a little damp and cold from being

outside for so long, and standing ten minutes in my underwear while Zebulon fleeced me hadn't helped. I picked up Todd's bag, the tapes, and the rain-soaked Chinese takeout box. I put the takeout box and the tapes in the backpack, bringing the box along because it's wrong to litter and because Todd may also have had some plan for the Rice Krispies and the toad that I didn't know about. Once I had repacked everything, I made my way over to a stairwell, noticing that I was on the Pineapple level. Not that it mattered—I wouldn't be coming back to the Pineapple level after the show—but I thought if I *would* have had to return, the Pineapple level would have been an easy one to remember, pineapple being such an interesting fruit.

A few freaks had set up camp inside the stairwell, and it had so much secondhand smoke coursing up it that I felt like I had stepped inside some gigantic bong. A guy on one of the steps about halfway down was reading a copy of *Lord of the Flies* with a flashlight. He looked wasted, the combination of a pig's head on a stick, marijuana smoke, and LSD not agreeing with him. When I'm tripping, man's inhumanity to man isn't my cup of tea either. That's stuff better left for rainy afternoons in the dorm. Somehow, at those times, a few "little-uns" being set on fire and a fat kid getting his glasses smashed aren't as shocking.

"Hey," I said to the guy.

He looked at me, snapped the book closed, and fled down the stairwell.

"Sucks to your asmar," I shouted, happy with my joke.

I had been hoping to ask the guy if he had an extra ticket, since his book was so enthralling, but I heard the door slam on the Banana level, and he was gone. It didn't worry me as much as it might have. Tickets had a way of showing up at Dead shows—that's half the karma of the experience. I just had to figure out how to make the kind of friends who were going to lay tickets on me. I passed a few more groups of people who eased back and let me pass and another guy spray-painting a peace sign on the concrete wall. I would have stopped to compliment him on his artistic flourishes, but he hid his can behind his back as I passed. I got snubbed four times in four floors, each time making me a little more certain that I had to get out into the crowd before my luck would change.

On the ground floor, the stairwell opened up into the

courtyard, a paved area about the size of three football fields and lit by spotlights along the coliseum. It was wall-to-wall people, and music floated from various tape decks at once. I cataloged the bootlegs as I passed—Syracuse '88 (two stars), RFK '87 (one star—Jerry was leaning on the mike), and a sweet old Red Rocks tape that I would have given my left elbow to own. I followed the sound of the Red Rocks tape in hopes of both tracking the owner down and finding Todd and Walter. If Todd were around, he'd be searching out the good sounds, too. I needed to look for a ticket or scope out possible ways of sneaking into the building, yet I was having trouble concentrating, listening to that beautiful tape fold into the other tapes, luring me deeper into the swirl of people. The music faded as I got closer to the coliseum and momentarily disappeared altogether in the temporary business district, a row of makeshift booths built out of packing crates, sawhorses, and boards.

The vendors along the edge of the coliseum were buying and selling all manner of useful goods—T-shirts, yo-yos, earrings, washable tattoos, underwear, scarves, knitted hats, ecologically correct toilet paper, painted seashells, coffee cups, moist towelettes, and peanut butter sandwiches with and without psilocybin mushrooms. In the thick of the crowd, I spotted a guy who looked like Todd browsing at a booth selling Grateful Dead golf balls. He stood with his back to me, inspecting the merchandise and having a conversation with the vendor. He had short hair and Todd's way of standing off from the booth in order to make palming a couple of freebies less conspicuous.

I was so happy to see someone familiar that I pushed my way through a group of Hacky Sack players in the throes of competition. They gave me a little of that "Easy, dude, where's the fire?" patter and let me by only after I had picked up their sopping-wet sack, which had ricocheted off my leg and was half floating in a puddle. They didn't ask me to join them, but sometimes that happened, especially when I had some dope to share or some peanut butter sandwiches to sell. Still, I don't generally go in for sports that make players look like Irish clog dancers or where I can get hurt just by the mismanagement of my legs. I came up behind the guy I thought was Todd and gave him one, two, three slaps on the back. One of the golf balls leaped out of his hand and landed in a puddle on the pavement. It would have had a hard time missing the water, the puddles outnumbering dry spots by about six to one.

"Can I help you?" the stranger who looked like Todd turned around and asked me. Color me stupid.

"Case of mistaken identity," I said, picking up the golf ball and wiping it off with the sleeve of my blazer. Some of the orange and green psychedelic coloring wiped off, too, but I didn't point that out. It had obviously been inked on with highlighter pens by the guy who was selling them—not a bad business idea but liable to go south on a rainy day. I handed the ball back, colored part up.

"Case of what?" the guy asked me, looking at me closely. He put the ball in the pocket of his windbreaker.

"Mistaken identity," I said. "Happens all the time."

"Sure." He looked at my face and down at my shoes.

The guy seemed out of place somehow with his short hair, windbreaker, and creased smile, not like Todd after all, not like anybody. His tie-dye shirt appeared to have actually been folded and stored in a drawer, and his shoes had double-knotted laces—two things that made me think this guy was at best a weekend Dead Head, an escapee from some institution like myself, or at worst a rent-a-cop in disguise. Already I had noticed a bunch of freaks handcuffed to a chain-link fence in front of the parking garage, attached there, no doubt, to keep the contraband trade down. Sometimes rent-a-cops felt like they had to put on a show in order to keep us poor freaks in line. It was kind of sad since you couldn't rein in a pure heart, but they were getting paid, and that probably made them happy. I saw a bunch of NEED TICKET signs, but I had yet to see any that read HAVE TICKET, which meant the jackasses were pinching scalpers, too.

The golf ball guy looked at me looking at him and, if possible, became twitchier than before, his fingers playing an imaginary piano. Scary as he was, I wondered if he was interested in trading his ticket for my Stillwater tie. I figured if he turned out to be a narc, I could just run. We were in a crowded-enough area that he would have trouble following me without splashing through a few puddles. Just as I was about to open my mouth, his hand shot up into the air at a forty-five-degree angle. At first I looked at the hand and where I thought the hand was pointing. Maybe the guy was hailing a jet. Maybe he had had some kind of muscle spasm.

"*Heil!*" He clicked his heels together, making a little mustache under his nose with his other hand.

At first I didn't get it. The Hacky Sack from the guys I'd barged into earlier splatted into mud a foot away and speckled my pants. A group of girls nearby stopped their gyrations and laughed into their hands, and a circle of old-fart freaks—Zebulon Nash types—wheezed out of their noses and choked out a few hee-haws. It was the Stillwater handshaker suit that was making everybody cute. The golf ball guy might have resembled a cop in his sublime details—his twitchy eyes, good posture, ironed shirt—but I resembled one in my clothing choice of blazer, tie, and khakis. The security guards in the area were all wearing blazers with the word SECURITY stitched over the pocket. They were all also wearing oxford shirts and ties. The difference between the Freedom Security uniform and my suit was that mine had seventy-five percent less polyester and the Stillwater crest stitched on my pocket. I also didn't have a flashlight hanging from my belt and I wasn't herding cars into a neat little row in the parking lot, but that didn't stop the small crowd from getting their laughs at my expense.

"Make love not war," the Lord of the Hacky Sack crowed, picking up the sack that had gotten mud on my pants.

"Look at the little midget fuzz," the biggest of the old farts said.

"You don't understand . . . " I pleaded.

What a carnival of errors this day had become. How could they have made such a mistake? If they had looked only a tiny bit closer, they would have seen signs of my freakhood in the pot-sensitive grains of my skin and the itch of my eyeballs. My mission in life was to promote peace and harmony and to get wasted. Over the course of two years, I had ingested an estimated six hundred thirty-eight bong hits, seventy-two hits of acid, several grams of coke, and more than my fair share of the supply of quaaludes Kenny J. had borrowed from his mother. I'd been to forty-five Dead shows and had eighty-seven bootleg tapes, sixteen tie-dye T-shirts, and a ceramic bank that looked like a turtle (which is some kind of hippie symbol, though I'm not sure of what). If the signs of commitment weren't written all over me, then something in the universe had gone terribly wrong.

"Hey, man, sell me your tie," the golf ball guy said, getting the old guys rocking back and forth again.

He had at least quit saluting, but he wasn't letting me off the hook entirely. Very faintly I heard strains of the Red Rocks tape again, "China Cat Sunflower." The old guys went back to telling each other some story that involved cocking their elbows in strange directions. The golf ball guy was getting ready to make another joke, but he had lost the attention of even me. Freaks don't hang on to their focus very long, especially old freaks. Something in the brain chemistry eroded their concentration and made them drift away on the slightest waft of sensory input.

"Excuse me," said a voice from behind the golf ball guy.

A short, frizzy-haired hippie, balding on top and wearing a flowered smock, tapped the golf ball guy on the shoulder. He looked for all the world like Art Garfunkel, and boy, was I surprised to see Art Garfunkel standing before us selling not just golf balls but also cup holders and mouse pads. He had clearly never given up being on tour, and he hadn't really given up music since he was surrounded by it, and from what I could tell, even though he had to deal with the occasional kleptomaniac and keep his vending license in order, he was still happy after all these years—or crazy, I forget which. Either that or the guy was just a big fan of Art Garfunkel, which seemed less likely. Art tapped the shoulder of the guy with the Windbreaker a second time.

"Excuse me," he said a little louder.

He was excessively polite for an ex–rock star/business-man who was about to confront someone for ripping him off.

"What?" the golf ball guy asked.

I wondered if it was wise to be standing there with a guy who steals golf balls from a gentle hippie vendor and a gentle hippie vendor who can't sing harmony. Todd and I were guilty of theft, sure, but we stole from the infrastructure and gave to the poor dudes on our floor, providing them with French onion dip on TV nights and Pez dispensers to get through their Latin sections. Mr. Windbreaker hadn't even bothered to pick up enough Jerryism to get through the day undetected, and that was sad to see, a guy with no natural talent. It took a few shows for the newcomers and the narcs who imperson-ated them to get the right attitude, the right look, the wider-than-usual pupils, the facial hair, the thinness that made older and more committed Dead Heads seem like they had climbed mountains in Tibet before arriving at a show. I wanted to reach out and wrinkle him and teach him some basic protocol: Never wear clothes that you would wear to a polo match, never talk to someone unless you want to get them high, never buy golf balls colored with highlighter pens.

Narcs infiltrated a show, mingled, and busted people for just about everything: drug offenses or scalping or indecent exposure (which had happened to Kenny J. once). I knew a guy who had fallen out of scaffolding and landed on Bobby Weir, getting himself arrested for assault.

The golf ball dealer noticed me sidling back and tapped into his yang side. I got the distinct impression that Art was taking me for an accomplice to the theft of his poor merchandise and saw my edging back as a way to do more injustice to his business. I pointed off toward where the Hacky Sackers were still doing their jig and watched Art turn to look and then turn back. Old Art yelled, "Don't move a muscle," but I moved them all, hightailing it out of that scene as fast as my little legs could carry me. Sometimes escape is a direction, like up, down, or sideways, and it's wise to follow the impulse as far and as fast as it takes you. I bobbed and weaved through knots of freaks with such gusto, the only thing missing was musical accompaniment.

And then I found that, too. Once my heart started settling down, I found and followed the strains of Jerry's voice and the Red Rocks tape again. The music lured me past a row of vendors and through a curtain of icy rain pouring down off the slanted roof of the coliseum. I passed a couple of pillars, and then the trail led me outside the beam of the spotlights, where it was much darker, and I had to stand still for a minute to let my eyes adjust. I knew if I was going to find a ticket, I was going to have to explore some potentially unfamiliar territory.

I picked my way over a group of female bodies lying flat on the pavement chanting some sort of garble. They were being watched by four old farts, one of them telling the others a story that had his whole body wrapping around itself, hand over hand, foot over foot. He wasn't so much narrating as dancing, and I could tell he had gotten his soul wrapped up in what he was saying. The other three were giving their attention to the women's breasts, which looked like a small mountain range rising from the pavement. The guy telling the story hadn't yet figured out that the enthusiasm his friends were showing wasn't for him. He was really leaning into the details, drawing them out. The four were probably old friends who'd heard each other's stories a few times before, the guy in the center being their version of Kenny J. They all looked like they were fucked up, too, and attention might have been hard to come by. Whatever it was, they were taking up the room between another pillar and some people lined up to go through the security check who just might have tickets to sell.

"Excuse me," I said, lifting my hands out of my pockets. Since I was in their airspace, I figured I ought to send the old farts a signal.

All of them turned around and exposed their serious, doglike faces. The storyteller stopped in midsentence. He had the oldest-looking face of all of them. It was as if his eyes had known better times and had experienced better drugs before the world had changed and started to mock the ideals of his Buddhism-loving, dope-smoking, protest-attending youth. He had a tattoo on the inside of his right arm. All of his friends had tattoos, Harley-Davidsons and one Skull and Roses. The storyteller noticed me standing behind him and swept his knitted hat off the top of his head and clutched it to his chest.

"I'm terribly delighted to make your acquaintance,

Lord Fauntleroy," he said without the slightest trace of irony.

He shouldn't have removed the hat. He was almost as bald as a cue ball, and static electricity made what hair he did have stick straight out. The guys around him laughed and knocked each other with their long upper arms. Laughter made their entire bodies jerk and their faces contort. I tried to laugh, too. Since I'd arrived at the show, my suit had made the most serious people edge away. Whole pockets of freaks took one look at me and darted around the nearest corner, like the power of my outfit was going to suck them into spending an afternoon on Wall Street, turn them into junk-bond traders with two kids and a wife and house in Connecticut. You'd think they'd take themselves more seriously than that, have a little more self-esteem, recognize that a suit was just a suit.

"Hey, man, could you get me a date with the queen?" one of them asked.

"Don't you be talking about his mother like that," one of Bald Head's friends said, and they all started thumping their knees and smiling so tight it looked like their faces were going to break in half.

Their laughter may have had more to do with the acid they had dosed than with me. Drugs are like that. They connect the people who are on them and isolate the people who aren't. I'd seen freaks laughing their heads off at the soles of their shoes or the rain coming down or the dimples in a golf ball, not noticing that to sober people there wasn't anything funny. I'd gone crazy myself once watching an old videotape of the atomic bomb, oohing and aahing over the beautiful, graceful blooms of the mushroom cloud, completely oblivious to the face of tragedy I was looking into and seriously bumming out when a teacher came by, thumped me on the shoulder, and told me to quiet down. Standing outside of the circle of the old dude's hilarity made me feel a little wistful, like I had grown up and they were the innocent, poorly managed children. It was embarrassing to be the grown-up, and I wished someone would pass me a jay.

Most of us had ways of losing the stress of our day: by coming home, popping a beer or a Coke and succumbing to a half-assed sitcom, by getting all fired up about the "Red Socks" even though they lose every damn time. People are crazy, but craziness is what can lead a person to a higher place. Every damn thing is a religious experience—you just have to draw people's attention to it and make them notice it.

The hippies wheezed and snorted and rocked their shaggy heads and the world split into atoms. It was sad. But the separateness was true in a way that made it less sad. I was not my mother's son but the assemblage of a hundred tiny molecules that had first found shape accidentally, coincidentally, and without regard to acknowledged paternity in the space of her womb. True unity starts with true isolation, which itself is the birth of individuality. People have to see themselves as things separate from the machine before they can see themselves as part of it. That had been some of the wisdom Zebulon had laid on me when he robbed me in the parking garage, when he told me to pull myself together, that it wasn't like he was going to kill me or anything. Zeb and I had shared a few moments with each other, but the guy was no buddy, more like a wise devil.

"How much?" I suddenly asked the group of hippie octogenarians having the time of their life at my expense.

"What?" one guy answered.

"How much would you give me to take care of the suit?" I asked.

They held a small conference, trying to figure out what I meant, coming up with a number, or a bid, or whatever the hell they thought it was I wanted. I could tell they were stunned by my voice, which was more hysterical than I meant it to be. Deep down, they weren't bad guys, and they may even have individually pitied me in my overdressed state, but like the golf ball guy, they just couldn't show it in front of everyone else. The storyteller fingered his lip, and one of the other three pulled out two quarters from his pocket. They offered me the quarters, a set of plastic juggling pins, one gold earring, a three-quarters-full bottle of peach schnapps, tickets for the upcoming show at Madison Square Garden, and the storyteller's wool hat before even hearing about the trick I was offering to perform. They were clearly guys who liked to be entertained, and they were still sober enough to figure out that I meant business. I settled on the peach schnapps.

"Perfect," I said, taking the bottle and unscrewing the lid.

The liquid had congealed around the threads along the top, and one of the old farts leaned in and helped me remove the cap. His gentle way of explaining his technique made me wonder if he had grandkids at home that he had to help with opening jars. Once we got the top opened, I poured the peach schnapps onto the sleeves of my handshaker suit. The smell of peach mixed with alcohol assaulted the air. I'm not much of a drinker, more of a vomiter where schnapps is concerned, so it didn't bother me using up what was left of the bottle for my experiment.

"Anybody got a light?" I asked when I was finished.

Nobody moved.

"This is a trick, right?" the guy who had offered me the gold earring asked.

I didn't answer, and someone reached across with a lighter already lit. I took it from the outstretched hand and held it up to my face, so close that the heat warmed the end of my nose and my eyes crossed as I stared at the white-blue center of the flame. The lighter must have been a new purchase because there was enough butane left to produce four inches of heat. Everyone watched the fire as if it were the first fire and we were a bunch of cave people. I moved more deliberately than I had moved all day, concentrating my movements like I had learned to by smoking dope, doing one thing at a time so as not to crowd or panic the brain. The old farts watched with their mouths open. I took the lighter and waved it gently, about six inches under the arm, until first one sleeve, then the other, smoked and hissed. When the sleeves began to burn, it looked like I had two trained squirrels wearing sequined orange-yellow dresses dancing along my arms. I held my hands out to either side to make myself bigger and to let the flame grow.

"Holy Jesus," one of the old guys said.

At first, the old farts continued to just stand there, their expressions blank, but once the blaze got rolling, they got excited. One guy got down on his knees in front of me, his face awestruck and as wide open as a beam of light.

"It's a trick," the earring guy told everyone else, but he didn't sound convinced, and no one else gave him the validation he was looking for.

And then, like every other time I had torched something, the whole spectacle got ahead of me. Before I knew it, the flames crawled up my back, and I began to feel hot and itchy through my shirt. I had a second to think, So much for double-wool blends, before one of the old farts ran around in a circle yelling, "He's on fire!

He's on fire!" attracting an even bigger crowd of people. Most of us are born hoping to someday be the center of attention, a saint, and carry a message that will transform the world and be remembered after the span of time has drawn to a thin trickle. I had no knowledge of what my mission was, and that lack of knowledge fueled a fire in me that I couldn't put out, a desire to deliver myself to the world anyway, empty-handed and potentially shallow. I was a candle on a birthday cake, singing a song of myself, and for a flicker, all I had wanted was nearly there in the eyes of the world.

If I'd only been a little more careful about picking the group of people to demonstrate in front of, then I might have had less reason to panic at the end. The ancient traces of LSD and THC and God knows what else swimming in the old farts' systems had left them too slow to react or give me room to dive for a puddle. They were either having flashbacks, visions of their draft cards and American flags igniting in their heads, or they had gone into cardiac arrest and were mistaking me for Moses with the bush. In addition to the visual spectacle of burning arms, a noxious black smoke was rising from my sleeves, making me light-headed with the fumes. In

Tibet, I once read, there were monks who knew how to spontaneously combust. They meditated on their anger and up they went. I felt like one of those monks or like a beacon burning on a dark shore, beckoning lonely wayfarers. In the background, I could hear the Red Rocks tape, beautiful and mysterious, quiet and soft.

The ecstasy of my self-immolation, like so many of my other attempts at a religious experience, ended when I heard Jerry's gentle voice and realized I had been, in the words of Dr. Keller, the school counselor, "violent as a direct reaction to shame" again. I had been trying to pull a Sweeny, a trick named after a guy in my chemistry class who had gotten too close to a Bunsen burner and turned himself into a blue-blazered phoenix. It took a long time to become a saint, another twenty or thirty incarnations, and I was definitely a first-timer on this planet.

"Where's the fire?" I heard someone yell.

Out of the dark, a woman with an Indian print skirt and long, scraggly gray-black hair arrived with a fire extinguisher. She was one of the chanters who had been lying on the ground earlier and, from the looks of it, the leader of the coven. She slapped toward me in her Birkenstocks and sprayed a flume of toxic waste in my direction.

The fire hid like a timid kid afraid to show his face in kindergarten. I stood there humbled, as did the old farts, not so much by the power of the fire but by the power of the woman who had put me out.

"Men!" she muttered, patting down my jacket to make sure the last sparks were quenched. "Men and their stupid fire rituals."

The coven gathered around to get a closer look at my doused state. Some of them were young, not much older than me, and beyond the stench of the burned suit and the chemical smell of the fire extinguisher, I could make out a waft of sandalwood and patchouli. I had expected a scolding, but they just looked me over and left me sitting on the pavement. The blazer, despite the scorching, kept its shape. It was a little darker on the sleeves and missing the coat of arms, which led me to believe that Zebulon had made a horrible mistake in not taking it when it had been offered. Sweeny's blazer had held up, too, which just goes to show that it's worth going for the more expensive blends. In my experience, polyester sucks.

After a few minutes, the women moved on, dropping flower petals on the ground around me as they passed in a single-file precession. The group of old farts hobbled somberly behind them, their heads bowed, too, and another group followed them, young white guys with half-assed dreadlocks. The doors of the coliseum had opened, and the entire ocean of Jerryites, the small knots and the bigger groups, untangled and formed into a great line that passed before me. People glanced my way, and in some faces I saw pity, but I could also see behind some looks a satisfaction that came from knowing that it wasn't their number that had come up but mine. I felt panic rise in my heart the way a jolt of electricity lifts the clinically dead off the table during an attempted resuscitation and drops the body down again with a greater heaviness than before. There was nothing I could do. I had played the game to the end. I had not earned myself a ticket to the show. The courtyard emptied out slowly, and I heard one last strain of the Red Rocks tape, "Scarlet Begonias," before that, too, wafted away.

Then began an awful keening, what sounded like a pack of coyotes but what in reality was the mournful cry of those who, like me, had arrived without knowing how they were going to get in and were being denied the Promised Land. One woman with braids held up her lighter and let the flame gleam in the darkness.

Then, in a shaky voice, she began to sing a requiem for us in our abandoned state. She was off-key, but she had a deeply sincere message. A couple people joined her, and within a few minutes, a vigil was organized. Seventy or more people gathered to hold hands and sing "We Shall Overcome" in front of the gates. I was tempted to join them. I had acid in my pocket, and I could sing, and yet I had seen storm clouds in front of the parking garage and knew that worse was out there waiting. Soon enough the clop, clop of the Horsemen of the Apocalypse arrived, the mounted police sent in to disperse us and send us on our way back to our own private hells.

Life for me at Stillwater was pretty much over. I couldn't imagine Todd welcoming me back with open arms. I had sold his acid, made his Rice Krispies soggy, and had probably been the one to kill the toad. I had burned my handshaker suit and would have to spend some of the money I owed him on a new one. He had done me a wrong, and the guilt that would grow up in him as the wrongdoer would make his apologies take the form of Nair in the shampoo bottle or Jell-O in the underwear drawer. All of these things occurred to me with a dull ache, as if they didn't really matter to me anymore, even my relationship to Todd. There was also the problem of my having skipped out in broad daylight in front of witnesses. The hangman team would cave if the headmaster, remembering that they were with me at lunch, started to interrogate them. With Knees out of the picture, my mother might fail to send in my tuition check in a timely manner, which meant my days of special treatment and privilege were over.

I still wasn't certain that life wasn't an empty roll of the dice anyway and that what came at the end was only a lack of wanting anything anymore. I still couldn't see my own fire too clearly, or understand my purpose, or why I was driven over and over again to act as foolishly as I did. People talk of light at the end of the tunnel, of great joy waiting for us on the other side. People talk of true believing as the acceptance of joy, and, oh, how I yearned for a belief in joy; almost every day, I yearned, and sometimes I felt it flicker in my heart. As I sat there under the eaves of the coliseum, out of the rain, I wanted to believe because Jerry had told me to believe, because believing was the only way I could make sense of what had come before and deal with what was to come after. I wanted someone to leave the door open for me, just a crack, so I could wander through it and know what a real miracle felt like. I thought of my better self and my worse self, and I felt some of my worse self walk out of me. A light shimmered in the puddle at my feet, a ripple on the water finally calmed by the end of the rain.

"What the Sam-H-E-double-hockey-sticks do you think you're doing?" Someone came up behind me with a flashlight.

A woman with bleached-blond hair wearing a blue blazer like mine (except polyester) stepped through the coliseum's emergency exit. In the darkness, I hadn't noticed the door, but now I was suddenly blinking in the beam she shone at my feet. I used my hand to shield my eyes. She reached down, grabbed my jacket sleeve, and stared directly at me. She bore no resemblance to any holy figure I had heard spoken of—no flowing robes or shimmering aura, more of a Nazi youth look.

"Are you parking lot or stairwell?" she asked.

She tucked her flashlight precariously under her chin and consulted her clipboard, turning the pages, looking at the list of names printed there for something she couldn't find.

"Do you even have a name tag?" she muttered. "Damn, this always happens when we get you kids from the college to help with the backlog." Behind her, I could see the procession of happy freaks inside the coliseum marching through the corridor in search of their seats. There was dancing and skipping and jubilation.

"Where's your name tag?" the woman demanded, and finally I confessed that I had lost it somewhere, along with my flashlight.

She clearly didn't approve of my on-the-job performance and made some comment about damaging uniforms that didn't grow on trees. She asked me my name again, and when I gave her one or two without the hyphens, she consulted her clipboard and then got frustrated. "Come further into the light," she snapped, and yanked me by the jacket into the coliseum. A couple of freaks glanced my way. A guy with a cigarette took one last drag and stamped out his butt. Once she and I were inside and the emergency exit door shut behind us, I pointed off toward the corridor and watched her turn her attention away from me to look. Just like Art Garfunkel, she followed the moving finger rather than keeping her eyes on the prize. The inside of the coliseum was gray and dimly lit, and the cement walls muffled the sound of her voice as she called after me to stop, wait, she wasn't finished with me yet, but it was heaven, all right. I recognized it.

DARK STAR

ACID TRIP—SOMETIMES GOOD, sometimes bad—always a story you burn to tell, if only to explain it to yourself. I once tripped so hard while home on vacation that I ran screaming down the main staircase into the foyer thinking that the striped Hudson's Bay blanket tucked into my underwear was a tail. Fucked up as I was, I couldn't tell the difference. Fortunately for me, the gardener was at work on a bank of peonies by the front door. He was a hell of a guy, presumably trained in Eastern meditation techniques since even in Japanese he was able to convince me that I was mistaken and that the blanket was just a blanket and my underwear was just my underwear. Without him, I might have been a goner—sent special delivery to the nearest funny farm and strapped to a bed. I'd heard stories, and not just from overly concerned teachers and health-care professionals either.

Once upon a time some government agency whipped up the recipe for lysergic acid diethylamide as a way to create hallucinations in people they wanted to interrogate, and that history always kills me, the machine handing over the goods to freaks. The Grateful Dead played accompaniment at the kickoff party and soon thousands and thousands of people were coming together and turning on, first one generation, the lucky one, and then another, and then mine, who listened to the music and blasted ourselves clean with the heat of our trips. Attending a Dead show and doing acid was as close to a Tantric experience as a white guy like myself was going to get, holy and purifying because it brought me together with others and made my individual dramas, my breathing trees and sprouting tails, swirl into the mass of other dramas. It brought the walls down. It opened the doors and let me know that way out there in the distance there was a light burning even though I was doing everything in my daily life to avoid heading toward it.

The chemical combination should only be for people who are serious about their spirituality, who crave the experience for more than the existential ha-ha and the weird colors. LSD is not a recreational drug, something I learned while trying to play table tennis and trip at the same time. Drugs as powerful as LSD and religion and music go together and have intertwined for all of history, since some caveman ate the wrong kind of mushroom and banged on a drum. No one, not even the most committed freak, the guy who wanders around barefoot in New York City or climbs mountains in Tibet, should go acid-crazy for longer than he needs to. The trick is to visit crazy and come back, tell the story, see God and unsee him again so you can go on believing in his mystery and become a prophet for those who are yet to come.

I had a journey to take, a vision I needed to have, emotions I needed to work out, and acid seemed like my bridge. The three Day-Glo hits of Donald Duck windowpane I had saved for the show had sat in our mini-fridge at Stillwater Academy for more than a month, preserved between two pieces of waxed paper and sealed with shrink-wrap. I had kept them hidden even though they might have purchased me an escape from my troubles, gotten me to my physical destination, and paid my way in much earlier. I had kept them hidden because I believed they were meant for me, and I was tired of everyone else taking my stuff or acting like my piece of the puzzle didn't matter. I found a quiet spot in the corridor between sections M and P, sat on the floor against the wall, and pulled the acid out of my blazer pocket. I could almost hear it speaking to me, telling me that my ride was a tongue lick away.

Freaks passed through the corridor on their way to their seats and left a dark track of melting footprints, widening as more and more of them passed, and thinning and melting away again when they were gone. I unwrapped the blotter paper and pressed the tip of my tongue against each of the three tabs. My synapses hissed, one, two, three. My soul rose like a bubble in an ice-cream soda floating to the top, the light and heavy changing directions. I knew I might wind up being carried out of the coliseum on a stretcher, but there was no backing away from destiny.

I stayed against the wall in the outer concourse, inhaling the smell of drying mud and rain and earth that had been transported from all over the Eastern Seaboard on the bottoms of Birkenstocks, Weejuns, Tevas, and Doc Martens, the basic shoe choices of all committed freaks. The dirt deposited on the Freedom Coliseum cement had mixed into the mess of cigarette butts and ticket stubs, an offering to a pagan god. I stayed against the wall long enough for the multitude's energy to move from the outside corridors of the coliseum to the inside and to pulse against the walls. The crowd became restless, the way it does when a show is about to start. People moved quickly and blindly. They were no longer looking for seats; they were looking for any way in they could find.

Just as I rose shakily to my feet, I was passed by a group of girls carrying tambourines, and I was swept along by the trails their shining hair made in the dim light. I found a door and headed up a flight of stairs after the group to the nosebleed section. The red railing sizzled under my hand, and the yellow paint on the risers made my feet float a half second before they hit solid ground. The first few seconds of my trip made me crazy happy. I was excited by everything I saw. I laughed at the stage's rotating purple gel lights, which slipped flat beams under my shoes and withdrew them again as I ascended. I laughed at freaks scurrying between the rows like rodents, and the happy bears on somebody's T-shirt. For a few seconds I laughed at myself for laughing, and then I took a seat, glad that I was alone, far from anybody I needed to explain myself to.

If Todd had been with me, he would have laughed the way he laughs when I get embarrassing. He would have shaken his head, which would have been my signal to sober up. But I wasn't obligated to honor Todd's code of coolness anymore. I could express myself as I pleased. I checked my—Todd's—backpack and unearthed the tape deck and began setting up to record just in case I was too fucked up later to get the details I wanted. The band hadn't started playing yet, but I wanted to catch the magic of row 177 or wherever the hell it was I was sitting. I wanted to record the buzz of the crowd during seat-finding time.

On a good tape, the first few seconds set the tone for the rest of the listening experience. All of my best tapes have great beginnings. To the untrained ear, the background noise can sound like a train yard, but shadows of music lurk in the hissing and squealing and popping, the white noise generally attending the first five minutes of any decent bootleg.

"Hey, you . . ." A guy tapped me on the shoulder and pointed down the row.

It took me a minute to figure out what he wanted since he was doing more finger stabbing than speaking, but then he pulled a ticket stub out of his shirt pocket and stabbed the printed numbers. He could still speak loud enough for me to hear because the crowd and the band hadn't revved up yet, but for some reason he was letting me translate the pointing instead. Knowing and practicing some kind of sign language has its advantages in a large auditorium setting when some of the crowd, dosed as they were, became more versed in Martian than English. I had forgotten that I actually had to sit where I was told to sit. A lot of details were slipping my mind, but this guy seemed unforgiving and unnecessarily excited.

"It's a free country," I started to say, but I didn't finish. Not only was I having trouble getting my mouth around the syllables, but the guy was a lot bigger than me, proportionally about what a redwood tree is to a willow branch.

I picked up my stuff and started to clear out. "Sorry." I held the microphone of the tape recorder up to my mouth. When I got a few feet away, far enough that he couldn't hear, I whispered his description into the deck. "Nazi with a ticket fetish," I said for the benefit of all future listeners. "Wearing a bad shirt."

Usually Todd did all of the recording and I just watched, wishing in the meantime that I could do it. Todd's not as experimental as I am in his conception of sound. He doesn't appreciate the extraneous noise as much as I do—the machine-gun rattle of the reels of the tape; the whine of the auditorium seats; the murmur of conversation; the tinkle of the dozen or so girls just a few rows up with their tambourines and another dozen closer in with skirts and hats and boots with bells; the ventilation system wheezing and choking and toking on the smoke-filled air; the screams and shouts of some happy or overstimulated freak with good drugs; the first and second and third clap of people who think they have seen something onstage and think something is about to happen but who are wrong on both counts; and the coliseum itself, at capacity, digesting its bellyful of people. On the tape I was making, I recorded my footsteps in the aisle and more description of the guy with the ticket. He was a seventies-era Donny Osmond type with big lapels and hair that bounced up on top and hung straight at the bottom. These kinds of details fleshed out the tape, gave it more than just the usual number of layers Todd's tapes had, getting me that much closer to my holy grapefruit.

"He's wearing bell-bottoms," I whispered into the microphone.

I was trying not to crack up, but I did anyway, and I think the guy noticed what I was up to because when I looked back, he was staring and his finger was raised in a semipoint at my recording equipment. I hurried away, placed myself, and got displaced a few more times until I found a seat that no one else seemed to want, belonging in all likelihood to some poor schmo who had come down with the flu the day of the show or had been too fucked up outside to find his way in when the time came. Even if he was one of those guys handcuffed to the chain-link fence, I was in his debt. I put my gear down on the floor and mentally adjusted to the altitude. In another hour, so much smoke and haze would drift into the atmosphere that I wouldn't be able to see the stage or the floor, a hundred miles down. In another hour, I would just be able to see the glowing outline of the band produced by the spots hanging from the trestles overhead. I felt like I was going to fall off the side of the world. A whole gang of people who had come together took up the rest of my row, and they passed a goatskin bag among them. It was only a matter of time before they got messed up enough to forget that I wasn't one of them and handed the bag to me. I was thirsty and a little hungry, too, the Cheetos I had had back at the Stillwater station nothing but a partially digested memory. The people in my row looked like solid Jerry's kids all right: floppy hats, tie-dye, old-fashioned values. Sometimes freaks might seem a few centuries out-of-date, like the guy with the big lapels, but they had definitely brought a better time and place up to the present with them.

None of them chased me away, for which I was thankful. Some of them stood on the stairs, but it looked to me like they wanted to stand. If you have to be trapped in a confined space with sixteen thousand people, pot smokers are the kind to do it with. This gang and I devoted the next fourteen minutes to getting the band onstage—a ritual among freaks, performed by banging on a knee or a seat back or clapping until your hands hurt. One time, I made the unfortunate mistake of going to a less-slow-moving concert with Kenny J. Just as we were easing into the dope we had smoked, the band ripped up onto the stage, picked up their guitars, and smacked the audience with something that sounded like earwax remover. I thought for sure it was one of Kenny J.'s practical jokes, that we had shown up at a pneumatic drill convention. I was more conditioned to Jerry's method: waiting for the crowd, easing onto the stage, doing a couple of mike checks, and letting Bobby say something unintelligible to the audience. I had gotten used to standing up for ten minutes, waiting to see and then seeing, and then pulling out a lighter and holding it up until the butane went dry. After my trip with Kenny J., I vowed never to go to another kind of show again, although I have to say crowd surfing was fun, something freaks could do, a little more slowly and a little more gently, to songs like "St. Stephen." I was contemplating this when Jerry lumbered onto the stage and the first notes of "One More Saturday Night" found their way to our section.

"Good choice, Bob," a guy who looked like Jesus—the beard, the beads, the soft, overly large pupils—yelled with his hands cupped around his mouth.

A row behind him, the shine actually leaped off the hair of a girl with black braids and I felt her buzz in my feet and just under my heart. The music and all three hits of acid swelled inside me. I usually take two hits, and the difference felt alien, much too clean and clear, like I was watching myself and there was going to be a written examination after the show. Since I could no longer write or even think in English, I'd have to come up with some glib details to pass. My first thoughts were of my step-father Knees—wherever he was—and I kept hoping he was listening to what the guy who looked like Jesus was yelling because it was what I would have yelled if I could have remembered how to yell. It confused me to consider that Knees wasn't sitting a couple of rows away, in his business suit, his hands resting on his thighs.

I plugged my ears with my fingers and watched the people in the rows in front of me dance, jump up from their seats, and gas it from zero to sixty in four-point-five seconds. I have always loved watching music without the sound. The dancers' elbows jerked toward their ribs, and their bodies rocked from the waist like they were being convulsed by a single, simultaneous epileptic fit or by a universal electrical shock. It takes a while for freaks to get their legs committed, another song or two at least, but they were definitely on their way. I let my fingers go—pop—on my ears and took another sonic hit of the music. It felt good doing that: silence, then Jerry, silence, then

Jerry inflating my eardrums and the inside of my head. The girl with the black hair whirled along the platform in front of me, and her Indian print skirt ballooned around her. Her braids flew out from her head like two magic wands casting spells. She was moving so fast that watching her was like watching the little dance of electricity on an old television set before the picture comes all the way on. I swear, even without my ears I could hear her crackle.

At first I believed I could trust myself, trust everything flung at my five senses. Then everyone on the other side of the coliseum stood up and pointed at me. Looking away, I turned toward the people down my row as the freaks there joked with each other and held each other up. They were a good-looking tribe, all decked out, not a single baseball cap or Windbreaker or pair of khaki pants in the lot. One girl a couple of seats away moaned and held up her hands, appreciating her knuckles and her palms. She was like a scientist studying the light side of a heavenly body to learn more about its dark side, taking peeks behind the curtain trying to figure out if the all-powerful Oz was just a carnival salesman or what.

My rational self was telling me that I needed to find

my stepfather Knees so that we could talk. We needed to have a long discussion to finish the discussion we hadn't had at Sam's lunch counter in September. Then I'd be able to tell him what a great guy he had been, how he'd helped me out with his long orations about personal responsibility and his occasionally boring stories about the banking business. The guy had recognized that I was careening down the jouncier double-diamond slope but laid no judgment on me even though he himself had stuck to the trails with the little blue squares. We came from a lifetime of differences and found a couple of similarities together. We were lucky. Not everyone was as lucky as we were.

Down below me on the stage, Jerry emitted a red blur of sound. A gel behind the stage haloed his springy hair, and the sound of his voice rose heavenward into the rafters. There was so little activity on the stage that it would have been easy to imagine that the band was asleep and that the music they were playing, which in the last few minutes had eased without pause into "Bertha," was just a collective dream we were all having. I sang along, holding up the microphone of my tape deck to catch my voice. I'd never sung too well and sounded even worse when recorded, but I was too fucked up to remember that. In addition, the people sitting next to me howled, and the girl with the hands obsession also sounded like her teeth were being drilled, so I knew this part of the tape would probably have to be dubbed over with commentary. After a while, I moved away into another row. I wanted to get a little closer to the aisle in case my panic button got pressed.

I once read that people who jump out of airplanes for the first time start running, even though they are running through air. Part of me was running when what I needed to do was wait for the chute to open. My hands started to get slippery and, like the girl I had moved to avoid, I couldn't look at them without going nuts. I could actually see my blood pumping into my fingers. I also felt heavy, like I had gained two hundred pounds in two minutes. I knew it was the acid, but knowing didn't help me separate illusion from reality. Todd didn't have my problem. "It's just the trip, it's just the trip," he'd say when the sky was going all kinds of different weird-ass colors, and then he'd sit back and pretend that the horrors of the universe were just out there to entertain him, but the girl in the seat a few rows over and I were chewing on the same nightmares, getting ready to pop out of our skins.

The music was the only thing saving us. The notes were golden threads that wove themselves into a wild tapestry of images, smells, and the floor wobbling under my feet. The acoustic ran as it always does, higher and lighter than the backup guitar; Jerry's voice danced another couple of notes above that. People in the crowd chose the line they were going to move to. There were girls fluttering through the backdrop of light, taking wing almost, and guys hunkering low to the ground, swinging their arms and stomping. The whirling-helicopter girl whipped past. I was just a step above an open riser overlooking the stage, and her hair and arms and skirt blew a breeze across my face. She made all kinds of gestures with her hands, wrapping them around and under each other like snakes on Erasmus's pole as she talked to me in signs. She repeated every note just as Jerry played it and transformed it into a movement of her body. Everything about her was beautiful: the way the light moved in her ebony braids, the way her shadow reduced the glare from the spots on the ceiling, the way she became the moon eclipsing the sun, the symbol of yin and yang. She was love, all right.

Pure, uncut, pay-with-your-soul, put-you-in-the-hospital love.

"Truth, beauty—" I said into the microphone in an effort to catch the moment before it slipped.

By the time I had finished reporting, she was gone. All around me, the crowd surged, an ocean that rose and reared before dashing itself against a rocky shore of ecstasy. We were stirred by the girl's appearance or the music rippling from Jerry's harp unstrung. No music the Dead plays has quite the same intensity as Jerry's music— not Bobby's booze ballads or blues. I liked "One More Saturday Night" but I worshipped all of Jerry's songs, and the ones that really made me fall on my knees were the ones with women's names: "Bertha," "Althea," "Scarlet Begonias," "Dear Prudence." When you thought about it, my mother was just like Sugar Magnolia: every kind of delightful and always dancing a Cajun rhythm. She wanted to be thrown to the wind, left to drift on the currents that moved her, while I had hopelessly, anxiously chased after her.

I got up and danced myself crazy in search of the whirling-helicopter girl, my pack flying out to the left and right of me, my tie and the tails of my jacket sucking up the air and making me fly. At first it was strange, being on my feet again. I couldn't quite stand up, but I wasn't exactly falling down, either. I smacked some guy with the microphone of my tape recorder.

"Look out, douche bag," he said.

"Sorry," I said into the tape, for posterity.

In all that thrashing around, I rapped about love with Knees—Jerry's love, my mother's love, and the whirling-helicopter girl's. I contemplated the love that loved people right up. We loved until we got to the point we were supposed to love, then we changed direction and loved somebody else. Love in its painful moments can be a taking back of everything you ever felt and in its good moments a giving of everything you have. You have to take it in, move on, not get stuck on love, but let me see you try. I was dancing the dance of love, moving close to one set of freaks and spinning away again, hurting myself, falling down, getting back up. I know I'm a maniac when I get started, but I don't owe much to the regulation lifestyle anyhow. Normalcy—normal families, normal schools, normal friends—had let me down.

Jerry belted out "Terrapin Station" next, and I danced up the stairs, risking uncertain pains of hell by getting tangled up in my microphone cord. I fell and made my nose bleed, then sat there laughing at the hard truth of cement stairs. This is why they call it the nosebleed section, I thought. The whirling-helicopter girl appeared from behind a concrete pole. "Hi," I tried to say while plugging my nose. Her hands flew out in arcs and rings and spirals. I took her hieroglyphics for her way of answering me. I made a few triangles and squares with my left hand in response. She spun away again, and I followed her, magnetically attracted to the electrons that had whirled off her body and her slashing dark braids. Down on the stage, Jerry never moved despite the throbbing and pulsing of the music. If you watched Jerry without listening, you couldn't decipher whether he was playing "China Cat Sunflower" or "Till the Morning Comes." Unlike the rest of us, he didn't seem to get bodily affected by his own sound. About an eighth of the crowd were sitting in their seats and watching, the same eighth that would have been just as happy with a black-light poster and a tape in their room back home—the Kenny J. types who can do celebratory sitting down. The rest were moving toward the strato-sphere like I was, like the whirling-helicopter girl was.

The real show was in the rafters and in the mind, and we were all rising up to get there.

"Hi." I tried to talk to the helicopter girl again after I had caught up with her.

I couldn't tell whether she knew I was following her or whether she was running away because of the energy of the music. She anticipated something more forceful in the last few notes of "Terrapin Station" and began swinging her arms and stomping her feet as she fled. You can do that—predict what's coming—if you listen to Jerry just right. The girl was a natural, a superacutely evolved and delicately designed higher-tuned species. Her loveliness sprang from the sharpness of the lines that trailed her, shot out from her like the tail of a comet. In less than two seconds, she was in the corridor behind the auditorium and I was with her. We danced like crazy in the extra space of the hallway without worrying about running into anything or knocking down a whole row of people like tipped dominoes. I did that once, at the Meadowlands—fell over while dancing and set one person against another until ten of us were tangled on the floor. The same clumsiness affected my steps into the next song. I was surprised by the violence of the music that Jerry was playing. Jerry was working out something, plucking the frustrated energy out of his guitar and messing with sixteen thousand fragile heads. Let it come, I told myself now that I had recognized it. Come what may.

Sure enough, Jerry played "Shakedown Street." *Bomp, bomp, bomp, bap-bap, bap-bap, bomp.* On the tape the bass sounded low, but live I could hear it in my appendix. *Bomp, bomp, bomp.* For part of the song, I danced with a water fountain and a piece of gum. The whirling-helicopter girl disappeared again, and I forgot her as best I could—not her glitter and her mystery but her bodily presence, her mortal self. One thing at a time, I told myself. Gum was in the drain of the water fountain—I was making it simple. Next to the wall. Above my feet. The wall. My feet. The water fountain. For a while, things got weird. The gum, I told myself. Somebody had chewed the gum and put it into the water fountain. That's how it had gotten there. Green gum. Greeeeeeeeeen gum. *Bomp. Bomp. Bomp.* "You just gotta poke around," Jerry sang.

I looked up. Everybody had drifted away. The shadows glinted. An arc of a watch swung toward a chest. Somebody checked the time, and I thought about the ways in which I had become evil and wrong to myself. I cared too much about just what happened to me. My ego held the reins and I could whine, whine, whine. We were all evil and selfish and trapped, and we do the best we can to pretend we aren't. *Twinkle. Badinkle.* Calm came from the music on the stage, Jerry's gift of acceptance, still giving. I thought about everything—not everything that had happened to me that day, not everything that had happened to me in my life. On the tape: gum, wall, water fountain—*bang*—but everything that could happen while I was thinking and thinking. *Poof.* Sonic pop of the brain. Never knew it could work the other way, that the music could suck you out as quick as you sucked it in.

On the tape, this part of the trip is dead air mixed with words. I had been too far away from the stage for the deck to capture the music, but the sound came back again as I began a search for the helicopter girl. She wasn't where I had last seen her, by the water fountain in the corridor, and she wasn't back near the doors. I promised myself I wouldn't panic, that I would just go back inside the auditorium and look for her there. I stood on the threshold, between out and in, for one whole song. I was surprised at how different the inside of the auditorium looked, as if I had been gone a hundred years and had come back to see a world that had changed, leaving me lonely for the one I had left. People were mostly sitting down. I could see faces, could actually concentrate on them and tell the difference between one person and another. The acid had receded, and for a while I was almost assembled, my parts all in one place. I found a seat, nodded to the guy with the lapels and the gang from the commune, and looked intently at the neck of the person in front of me as he tucked his hair under his pancake hat.

I recognized a hole in the semblance of the night—something missing. The band had stopped playing real music while Mickey Hart banged and banged and banged on his drums. I didn't record him. I had enough "Drums" and "Space" in my bootleg collection to fill up one whole shelf if I ever needed to. I tried to put the lost pieces together. The music had followed the tide of my trip out, and I was a little dry in the back of the throat, sore in my spine. I would have another wave of ecstasy, I told myself. Sometimes I got greedy for the fix acid put on my head. Sometimes I tried to force the action by inventing it. The stage wasn't a blur anymore. A bunch of balloons in a net hovered in the rafters. Long panels of sheer tie-dyed material swept over the scaffolding. A million gels splashed different colors on people's heads, on and off the stage. The band still hadn't moved from their prescribed spots. They never moved. Only Bobby moved. I had never seen any of the members of the Grateful Dead move besides Bobby, and there were times I wished he'd keep on moving and go.

Of the people onstage, Jerry was the least animated. He bent over his guitar and looked at the strings. He never looked at anything or anyone else; that guitar had all of his attention. He didn't bother looking at the other band members or the sixteen thousand of us looking at him. While I looked at Jerry not looking, the acid receded even more. I'm embarrassed to say this, but I sensed weariness not just off the stage but on it, too, as if Jerry were feeling his humanity and his moving fingers were the only things keeping him going. Concerts get slow once the novelty of getting to one wears off and the dope has been smoked and your feet are sore from dancing. The average climbers of Mount Everest don't dig sucking from an oxygen bottle, working their way around seventy or eighty crevasses, and having their head and eyeballs ache from altitude sickness, but they do dig catching a view of the world below them.

The seat tortured my gluteus maximus, and the group with the goatskin bag went back and forth to the bathroom, making finding legroom tricky. Still, I knew it was the necessary suffering of a good trip. The rest of the band was taking a metaphoric coffee break while Mickey was doing all the work, banging on those drums. Jerry looked at his guitar, and the gels over his head switched to green. And how many times had he done this, anyway? Ten million?

The people sitting next to me began to annoy me. One of them, a tall guy with red hair, worked with a penknife to pull the plug off a phosphorescent-glow necklace. Once he had gotten it off, he let all the chemicals inside run down his legs and gave himself electric clothing stains—junior freak behavior, if you ask me. That stuff doesn't come out even with extra-strength Tide and hot water. He and his friends spread it all over themselves and the people sitting in front of them, and pretty soon the whole row had electric spots all over them. One girl freaked. She started screaming and crying and claiming that she could see her bones. It did look like the chemicals were glowing from the inside of her body instead of from patches spread over her jeans, but she was overdoing it a little, pouring on the drama. Some people get a little purple on drugs, think they are far frailer of mind than they really are. My poor, tripping head kept receding out and out and out, so far out I felt like I was looking at the whole mess on a postcard: the rabid fans and what they had fallen for, the spectacle and insincerity, the rites and rituals that failed to summon up one damn concrete entity.

"Get on with it," the guy who looked like Jesus yelled down to the stage.

I couldn't get over not getting a fix on my head. It was going to take a miracle for me to fall back into the scene. The band started playing together again, picking up the second half with "Touch of Grey." The back of my head had lots of sad wisdom for me. *Put up with what gets you down*, my head said. *Quit trying to fight fate. Some people are born to lose.* I heard my mother's voice, though my mother had never said these kinds of things to me. I wanted to stop thinking about myself, but every time I tried, I was back where I had started. You have to think about yourself to stop thinking about yourself, and I couldn't get out of the loop. No helicopter girl came along to save me, although I searched the rafters for her. My stepfather was with me again. He didn't talk; he just tapped his thigh to "Not Fade Away." I did all the talking. The concert went on without us. "Knees," I said, winding up the way Walter had wound up, with the energy and innocence of somebody who still expected others to listen. "Thank you for taking me out onto the lawn in Maine and putting a croquet mallet in my hand. Thank you for giving me info on the sixties and for sticking with me and my mother as long as you did." I kept thanking Knees until, after a while, I couldn't do it anymore. I started hitting up everyone within hitting range for more acid.

"Please," I said.

People died at Dead shows but not in the way I thought I was going to die—not from underconsumption or a deficit of good drugs. In the late eighties, a couple of Dead Heads were killed when a fence they were climbing collapsed. Eight hundred other Dead Heads were climbing the same fence, and in their enthusiasm to make it over, they had forgotten about gravity and about what can happen when a fence falls and leaves some people still coming over the side. On the other hand, a couple of years ago three Dead Heads at an outdoor show climbed into a tree for a better view and were hit by a bolt of lightning. They lived and the rest of their lives were spent knowing that some of us can be spared, that goodness and mercy existed. And which was harder? Fate or a world of hard-hearted justice where forgiveness miraculously plucked you out of harm's way and gave you no way to say your thanks? I wasn't going to die of my mental drought and a lack of acid in my system, but I felt like it. The first wave of my trip had been a joy, the second sorrow, the third pure oblivion. Jerry played "Friend of the Devil" and "Uncle John's Band" and "Man Smart, Woman Smarter" and didn't seem to be in the mood to quit. Near the door down below me, a group of security guards gathered and looked like clouds rolling in. They readied their flashlights and watched the freaks dance.

I watched the coming storm until, from somewhere behind me, the helicopter girl spun into view and veered closer and closer to the red railing at the edge of the section. She had appeared there at the same time as the security guards, but at first I hadn't recognized her. She looked like she was dancing in deep water. Her revolutions had slowed, and every once in a while she lost her balance and tipped over entirely. She was still a counterweight to the Hitler Authoritarian types, and she still looked pure, but not as pure as when I had first seen her. No one else seemed to notice the rent-a-cops. The gang of freaks in my row pulled out another Baggie and rolled a last fat one for the road. All around me, seats were beginning to empty, people abandoning our part of the coliseum to get closer to the stage or to get a jump on the return trip. The risers still smelled of dope and sweat and patchouli, but the glow sticks had stopped glowing and the guy with the big lapels had moved on. I thought of him again and laughed. I don't know why he had become funny again, because he wasn't. Acid trips are hard and sad. Inside of me, I had fifteen different kinds of laughs waiting to get out: happy, sad, stoned, disgusted, mean, dorky, embarrassed, grumpy, sneezy, dopey, bashful, Donder, and Blitzen. Laughs of yin and laughs of yang. They all hurt.

I stood up and the helicopter girl fell down—not completely off the balcony, just onto the floor—and I started laughing harder. The helicopter girl laughed, too, grabbed her stomach, and kept on laughing. For a second I thought she was laughing at me laughing at her, but she wasn't; she was just laughing, which made me laugh. Pretty soon we laughed ourselves into deeper intestinal pain, and then she threw up. Her insides poured right out, and her vomit was as beautiful as a feathered wing brushing the air in front of her. The helicopter girl fanned a moss-colored arc across the railing, and vomit rained onto the floor below us in heavy, liquid plops. The freaks on the floor freaked. The helicopter girl didn't bend over and vomit the way someone less sure of herself would have vomited. She vomited standing straight up, turning herself inside out. The vomit missed hitting me but didn't miss hitting the security guards behind me, who had moved in closer to see what the commotion was about. And it wasn't just one convulsion. It was convulsion after convulsion of vomit launching itself into the atmosphere. It was difficult not to respond in kind, to vomit just for the sake of vomiting. A guard grabbed the helicopter girl while she was still emptying herself, and she yelled the first spoken words I had heard from her mouth all night.

"Let go of me, you fucking pig!" my beautiful vision of love screamed.

The security guard took hold of her under one arm.

He was a big though not completely confident guy. The helicopter girl, on the other hand, was a Hecate ready for a religious battle. She wiped her chin, stretched herself to her full height, and whirled around, threatening the first guard and a second who had joined him. She brandished one of her Birkenstocks, and for the first few minutes of the conflict, she seemed to have the better of her opponents. Her braids whipped around her head like two blue blades and caught the big guard on the chin. Her eyes glowed, and she backed up until the light silhouetted her. They closed around her then—more blue suits than freaks, a whole group of them with flashlights in their hands. They knocked me out of the way and started grabbing at her wild, beautiful arms and legs. They lifted her up off the ground, and her Birkenstock, the one she had used as a weapon, fell on the floor like Cinderella's lost slipper. She kept on fighting and spitting and drowning out the music with her shrieks and curses, but the guards now had the better of her, and for one awful second I thought they were going to tie her to a stake and burn her right there.

"Hey," I said, but no one seemed to hear me.

"That's not cool!" I shouted.

I wanted to tell them that this was a peaceful situation, that any kind of difference between us could be worked out calmly, with some mutual understanding, but the rent-a-cops didn't listen. They must have had to wear some kind of protective device under their suits to keep positive vibes out and the authoritarian bullshit in. Jerry was down onstage banging out good karma, finishing "Sugar Magnolia" and starting something I couldn't identify but knew was meaningful. The rent-a-cops didn't listen. They were tuned out, missing it, missing the directive of the music, the *wah-wah* of Jerry's guitar and the echoing current of anticipation in the crowd. No doubt about it, my mood had shifted. A deep separation existed between my last set of emotions and the ones I was feeling, like I was a helium balloon untied from my string. I suddenly knew what I believed in, the sanctity and seriousness of the mystery unfolding all around me, and I knew that I had to act on it, not let it be laughed at or let fade away.

"Move it, kid." The security guards passed by me, the weight of the helicopter girl suspended somewhat awkwardly between the two who had gotten to her first.

I wanted to reason with them, convert them, but

they were too far gone. The helicopter girl vomited one last time, covering the guards with the leftovers of her celebration: the mushrooms and red wine, the music-churned bile, the sodas, the eggs and breakfasts of eight days before, all dizzied in the froth of her stomach. She must have had a long prelude to the show, even longer than mine, because after she vomited, the life went right out of her. One second earlier she had been fighting—one shoe on, one shoe off, kicking, sinking between the two guards' arms as far as she could, slipping one arm out and then the other when they caught her again—and the next second she had given in, disappeared into the void behind her eyelids. I couldn't stand to see her go, sandwiched between the guards like so much limp lettuce. The security guards looked stunned, too. For one second the entire coliseum settled to silence, as if someone had pushed a Pause button or as if the action were part of a poorly spliced movie reel. For one second no one moved, no one coughed, no one breathed.

"This is a peaceful situation!" I insisted.

The security guards looked at one another. The helicopter girl's head dipped over the side of the big guy's arm. I picked up Todd's backpack and pulled everything

I could out of it: the tapes, the extra clothing, the dead toad. I littered the floor around me with stuff, some of it valuable, some of it that could have been sold if Todd had been around to find a market. I threw the stuff at the security guards, pelted them with it—the tops of their heads and their hands thrust forward to protect themselves—and then I started digging for more. At the bottom of the bag, I found the .45. The heft and feel of it in my hands made me forget all the other things I had thrown. I knew I had no choice. Todd had been right all along. It was time to let out the inner Snidely Whiplash and stand like a man. I aimed the gun at the bigger of the two security guards.

"Die, motherfucker," I said, more or less as an experiment.

"Whoa, there." One of the security guards, the one I was aiming at, realized what was happening. "This is a peaceful situation," he said, as if he had been listening after all. He let go of his end of the helicopter girl so that part of her dragged on the floor.

And then something else happened, a miracle really. Jerry began playing "Dark Star," and the crowd exploded with such energy, even the security guard who was approaching me was rocked back. Every single person in the coliseum suddenly rose to their feet and began screaming and shouting. Jerry never played "Dark Star," but, sure enough, the whole auditorium was jumping up and down and dancing and celebrating and just plain going crazy. The second security guard dropped the helicopter girl's legs and ducked out of the way of all the flying arms and rotating bodies of freaks in ecstasy. One or two of his fellow guards pulled their flashlights out, but so much had already begun to happen that there was nothing they could do. Who were these guys to say we couldn't dance, couldn't throw up, couldn't celebrate? I hated rules. I especially hated the rules that told me who I was supposed to be. I could have blown them all straight to bits, snuffed the life out of them.

I lifted the gun, but I couldn't pull the trigger. I couldn't. Maybe if I could have set it to stun, I could have pulled the trigger, but actually kill something? I couldn't do it. It was just like me to find the damn gun in my hand in the first place, a gun I wasn't going to use on anything. I was a fucking teenager, for Christ's sake. I had years and years to do my part in the world—why the hell did I think I had to do it that minute?

With everyone pushing toward the stage, I was able, through some wild combination of luck and effort, and thrashing, and yelling, to ditch the gun and pick up my recording equipment and one of the helicopter girl's Birkenstocks. Carrying my load, I both danced and ran, the security guards in pursuit. The acid made my brain slower and I felt my way through the crowd, moving as much on the ecstasy of the music as on my own legs.

Once inside the corridor, I found the emergency exit and escaped into the empty courtyard. The requiem freaks had gone home, apparently figuring out there is only so long it's wise to mourn on a cold November night. The rain fell in huge sheets and nobody stopped me or asked me where I was headed.

I held the Walkman in my arms close to my chest so it wouldn't get wet and hurled my way through the trash in the courtyard. Freaks can really make a mess when they put their mind to it. There was litter everywhere, whippet canisters, glass bottles, McDonald's wrappers, and old golf balls. I looked back, but no one was there. Water streamed from the roof of the overhang and soaked my pants cuffs and my hands when I reached out from under. I let my hands empty and fill again. There was a loud roar as if a spaceship were taking off from earth and I knew "Dark Star" was ending. Eventually I worked my way back to the Pineapple level.

Somewhere behind me was a girl limping around looking for her shoe. I wondered how I was going to get myself home, but I wanted to play the last few minutes of the tape back, just to assure myself it was all real. I heard Jerry, then the crowd, and then "Dark Star"—most of it, anyway, enough to prove that it had actually happened. I heard the sound of my own voice, breathing very hard, and the security guard who had almost caught up with me in the corridor shouting at me as he got closer, and his voice as he started to lose me again.

"Son," the voice said. "Now, son . . ."

Always behind that voice there is music, an undulating river, narrowing and deepening and flowing unstoppably toward the rest of my life. The Freedom tape is the best tape I ever made, three stars—"Bertha," "Terrapin Station," "Dark Star." It's a package, that tape, that distant voice that will not fade away.

AFTER

Freedom Coliseum was my last real hurrah—not the last time I would see Jerry onstage, but the last best time, though I had been too blitzed for most of it to recognize the history I witnessed until much later. After Freedom, enough things changed that made it easier to let go of the things that were never going to change: my over-sexed mother, disappearing fathers, propensity to vio-lence when made to feel shame, and desire to tag after guys like Todd rather than think for myself. The Free-dom Coliseum show was a turning point for Jerry, too. Though he finished out the fall and spring tour schedule and was on the road again in the summer, he had plans he hadn't divulged to any of us.

I was still thinking Jerry would go on forever. The night of the Freedom show, I put my tape into the breast pocket of my handshaker suit and tried to hit up other freaks for a ride home, but as everyone was still wigging over "Dark Star" and still in their private bubble, I was on my own.

Eventually I used a pay phone to call the headmaster. I had the digits memorized, my prankishness having once taken the form of nuisance calls. I didn't call Vonda because she wouldn't have picked up, and I didn't call Knees because he had left no forwarding address. The headmaster was unhappy to hear from me at 4:00 AM, and he almost didn't accept the charges. I was pretty fucked up at the time and I wasn't sure who I was talking to and I remember saying a lot of things that probably didn't make sense. In any case, the proctor eventually came and got me, but instead of taking me back to the school, he dropped me off at home, along with several packed bags full of tie-dyed underwear and most of my books and tapes. Apparently no one at Stillwater gave one iota of a second thought to my alumnus/donor potential.

For the next month, I lived at the Connecticut house with Vonda, our dog, Rufus, and my mother for the two or three days she was back from her book tour. Mostly I watched the snow fall and kept track of *Guiding Light* and waited to see if that Peck asshole was going to get back together with his psychiatrist ex-wife, his evil twin's former lover, or whether she was going to smarten up and ice the last version of him with the arsenic she had hidden in the drawer of her bedside table. I set a room up for myself in the pool house, with a lava lamp, my black-light poster, a few tapestries, and a bong. I had days where I missed the Poltergeist and Kenny J. and his crazy disappearing/reappearing ball, but mostly I was so burned out *Guiding Light* kept me going.

My mother's issue of *Playboy* hit the stands in January and she looked dynamite, her left nipple hardly sagging at all and her skin airbrushed a youthful pink. When she returned, teddy bear in hand, we joked about the things the photographer had told her to do to keep her chin up and stuff that got printed in the media about her later. We both got less talkative when the subject of Knees arose, the emotions that had divided us still tender. A Christmas card arrived in the mail about a week after New Year's wishing us the joys of a yuletide season with Knees' signature just under the Hallmark greeting. I sent him the picture I touched up with my highlighter pens at Stillwater, and that was the beginning of a correspondence that we mostly keep up.

While looking to score dope for the home supply, I also met a guy who knew Todd's brother. It was right before I was sent off to a place called Fissure Rock Early College, and I was nervous about the prospect of starting a new school and making new connections. He told me that Todd's father had been indicted for securities fraud and had hidden out in the Caribbean until he was extradited at Christmas, sent back for some jail time. I'm guessing Walt had an inkling of the nature of Todd's troubles, and what would come after. Todd must have confessed to Walt instead of me because of how wrapped up and crazed I was, more of a ward than a buddy, definitely not a sidekick in the fight against evil. Walt probably deserved the cape after all, since rumor had it Todd finished at Stillwater and went to Vassar, though I'd have to say, Walt was a fink for not tipping me off somehow to what was going down.

Then one day after I had started at Fissure Rock, I was in the basement laundry room of my dorm washing colored T-shirts and shorts. Some dude bounded down the stairs and asked me if I had heard the news. I was flustered enough trying to deal with figuring out how to put the soap in the machine and where to put the quarters, since they did the laundry for us at Stillwater and I was still a beginner. At first I didn't hear the urgency in the guy's voice. He proceeded to tell it to me slowly because I had a certain reputation, even at Fissure, even in my first weeks, as an emotional responder. He tolled the mournful bell. Jerry was dead. No more tours, or tie-dye, or sunshine daydreams.

I stood there holding my bottle of fabric softener against my chest, afraid to take my next breath. I wondered whether I wasn't responsible for the tragedy somehow, whether my unlikely decision to soften my clothes had upset the karmic balance of the universe. During his career, Jerry Garcia had survived comas, heroin addiction, acid tests, death threats from fans, and drinking bouts with Pigpen. But for some reason, that day, he didn't survive my decision to have fresher-smelling clothes.

I had never used fabric softener before, but like a lot of unsuspecting fools, I had tried using it to deal with the problem of unpleasant odors, scratchy towels, and static cling, things that hadn't bothered me that much before but then suddenly did. The tiresome little bear that stared smugly back from the label of the blue bottle

I held, the bear I would eventually come to call the anti-bear, turned out to be a perverse cousin of Jerry's bears, the ones that emerged from blotter acid and traversed the T-shirts and bumper stickers and tapes that soon became collector's items. His name was Snorkel or Sniggle or Sniffle or some dumb shit like that. He brainwashed the world with promises of fresher, softer towels, but what he was really doing was bringing down a hell and damnation of itching and sneezing, death, and the dark side of softer clothes that smelled like baby bottoms and pine trees.

There was a lot of subsequent freak grieving after Jerry's death, a lot of mourning for an era lost and despondency for a new world that seemed less sincere. I road-tripped to San Francisco to be in Haight-Ashbury for the grieving and Golden Gate Park for the memorial. I spent three days in a homeless shelter until I moved to the Hilton so I could take a shuttle back to the airport. The group sorrow cheered me up, but empty months followed in which I sat around and read and watched *Star Trek* in my room by myself. I stopped smoking so much dope so I could pay better attention. If you make a mistake as big as losing Jerry, it changes the rest of your life.

Ultimately, Fissure Rock Early College turned out to

be a place in the Berkshires rife with freaks like me, so many freaks that even the instructors and the administrators were freaks, not a tie or a suit jacket in the whole place. The parking lots were full of rusting Honda Civics and psychedelic Volkswagen vans. The classes had names like History of Transcendental Meditation and Jimi Hendrix 101, and the goal was to get kids too freaky for public and private high schools at least as far as an associate's degree. The place had the makings of nirvana for a guy like me. There were so many freaks at Fissure that I gave some thought to taking up homosexuality or Scientology as a sideline—until I found out that a lot of the freaks at Fissure had homosexuality and Scientology covered, too.

Nobody much cared who my mother was at Fissure Rock. There were enough other cases of poor genetic luck—the sons and daughters of disgraced politicians and the son of a woman who had accidentally removed her husband's penis in a boating incident. My problems seemed meager in comparison. My roommate was a guy from Pakistan, funny as hell, always laughing at my stupid rich American ways, but I could never understand a word he said and that was probably just as well, because it's easier to live with a guy if you aren't needing him so much.

The most beautiful thing about Fissure Rock, though, was that there were hundreds of girls. Every other person was a girl, and their underwear got mixed up with mine in the dryer and I had to knock on heavenly doors to return it. I found out I wasn't as backward in the girl department as I had always thought. I was no Steve, but they responded to my idiocy with kindness and affection. Thanks to my mother, I had a lot of technical knowledge, and that helped, and pretty soon I was chasing girl after girl, hoping to get with them just so I could hear them sing their arias.

Of course, Jerry's replacements rolled in. Soon the freaks at Fissure Rock were attending shows by bands like Phish and Ratdog, and at first I was resentful of the infidelity, seeing everyone who went that route as a sellout. But then, man, I got to listening and talking to other dudes and arguing over stuff. The music wasn't the same, not nearly as clear or finely tuned, but still there was a glint of something winding along, flowing into and out of itself. Even the tapes got replaced by burned CDs, little disks that would last forever. Eventually, with some dope and good company, I was carried away, too, and though I miss Jerry with all my heart, I am compensated by the loveliness of the world he left behind.